THE VIGILANTE'S AWAKENING

VOL. 5

Annie Winters
Tony West

www.anniewinters.com
www.tonywestwrites.com

casey shay press

Casey Shay Press
PO Box 160116
Austin, TX 78716
www.caseyshaypress.com

ISBN: 9781938150562

Also available in digital format.
eISBN: 9781938150579

Library of Congress Control Number: Pending

FIRST EDITION

Also by Annie Winters

The Vigilante's Lover Series

Writing as JJ Knight
The UNCAGED LOVE Series
The FIGHT FOR HER Series

Writing as Deanna Roy
Forever Innocent
Forever Loved
Forever Sheltered
Forever Bound
Forever Family

Learn about appearances and events at
www.deannaroy.com

For Annie's Vigilantes

Best fan group ever.

1

MIA

The door to the enormous vault in front of me is formidable. Twenty inches of steel. Dual combination wheels. Ten reinforced bars.

Black starbursts on the silver finish serve as testaments to other operatives' failed attempts to blow their way inside.

I will get the job done.

My watch buzzes lightly against my wrist. It's a timer. I have ninety seconds before the hired goon will come back around to this hallway. Less if the other goon at the security station notices that one of his monitors is displaying a recorded loop.

The clear green cylinder of explosives fits neatly into my palm. I plug in a display screen to one side, calculating blast volume and loading density. I estimate the size of the space. I only have a five-by-twelve hall and a ten-foot ceiling. We're underground. The last thing I want to do is bury myself alive.

I need a big enough explosion to compromise the door, but contained enough to avoid an injury. I have to stay close to confirm that the door is blown.

A blast that big in a space this small makes that complicated. I enter my data and set the parameters.

Thirty seconds.

When I'm sure I've got it right, I rip off the protective strip and attach the cylinder to the vault door. The device beeps its acceptance of my calculations. I pause and listen for footsteps or any hint that I've been discovered. Satisfied that everything has gone perfectly, I key in the initiation sequence.

Ten seconds.

Now to get out of the way. My outfit isn't helpful. I've had to play the part of the security guard's girlfriend, a high-maintenance type with a penchant for spike heels and bangle bracelets. I back up to take cover behind a concrete planter in the farthest corner.

The countdown gets to three.

Two.

One.

BOOM.

The blast hits like someone's shoved me backwards. Even with the reinforced planter in front of me, I slam into the wall. My head strikes hard against the plaster, and stars burst through my vision.

Damn it. Set it too high.

I shake my head, trying to clear the fog. Everything is black for a second. I try to force myself up in the awkward shoes. I can still salvage this. I just have to check the visibility of the vault and get out.

But I'm too dazed and moving too slowly. Strong hands grasp my arms on either side. I'm lifted up. Caught.

Damn, damn, damn.

There's a crackle of static and a voice comes through the intercom above. "That's enough. Clear the air."

The smoke and dust are instantly sucked out of the hall. The front wall slides open to reveal the control panel and my training director, AnneMarie Wash.

She is not pleased.

"Operative Morrow, this is your sixth failed attempt to open the vault without incapacitating yourself." She leans over the microphone and peers at me through the blast-proof window. "I think we're done here."

I wrestle myself loose from the two Vigilantes who pulled me from the wreckage of the vault wall. A crew has arrived to clean up the mess and prepare the testing room for the next attempt.

It will now be someone else's attempt.

"I can do it!" I insist, looking up at AnneMarie's severe black haircut, angled at her chin like a razor blade.

Her dark penciled eyebrows push together in annoyance. "Operative Morrow, we have five other Phase Ones who are eligible for this qualifying mission."

Jax steps through the side door, impeccable in a charcoal suit.

"But none of them look like the guard's

4

girlfriend," he says smoothly.

"Mr. De Luca," AnneMarie says. "How good of you to stop by and meddle. Going to throw your weight around?"

Now I'm fuming. Jax is a Phase Ten who is currently the acting head of syndicate. Everybody listens to him.

He's also my boyfriend. Well, more than that. There is an engagement ring involved. I just haven't accepted it yet. I want to be more than a bride. I want to be a badass.

"Jax," I hiss. "Please." I've told him I want to prove myself without his interference.

AnneMarie sits back in her chair. She's peeved he's here.

"Say what you've come in here to say," she grunts through the intercom. "But even *you* can't make me send an unqualified Phase One on a mission."

Jax leans against the wall, casually, as if they are having a watercooler chat. Nobody relaxes, though. Jax is formidable in his custom Armani, perfectly cut black hair, and that *face*. We've been together a year now and I'm still not sure how he achieves a constant level of perfect scruff.

Behind him, the crew dismantles the blasted vault door. At least it's open. I got that much done. But getting caught is worse than failing to blow it. Vigilantes must be invisible, always. No one even knows we exist. Not the government. Not law enforcement. Nobody. We must do our job silently, efficiently, and without mistakes.

After a long, silent standoff with AnneMarie, Jax speaks up.

"Perhaps if Operative Morrow is failing," he says slowly, "you should consider the quality of your training program."

AnneMarie's face flames red from her neck to her glossy bangs. She hadn't expected a personal attack. "I supervised her myself," she says. "Operative Morrow never showed exceptional aptitude for any skill sets requiring chemical precision."

I can see all my efforts to do this on my own going up in smoke. Jax is doing more than interfering. He's *threatening*.

"Jax, I've got this," I say. "She's right. All my testing showed I was more appropriate for strategy. People stuff. Not explosive stuff."

He turns to me, tugging his cuffs so that

precisely one inch shows from his jacket sleeve. I know this is a sign he's holding back his rage.

"You are the most talented Phase One this silo has ever seen." He turns back to AnneMarie. "This mission is nothing important and probably a waste of her time. But I do consider it a test of whether or not this training group will be allowed to handle our most promising Vigilante trainees in the future."

A young man in a brown Phase Two flight jacket rolls his chair closer to AnneMarie. He's been watching my failed attempts and resetting the equipment. He fumbles with a tiny clip mike.

"He's kinda right," he says into it. "After a blast like that, we should be taking her out on a stretcher. She's got exceptional control over her cranial and inner-ear functions. Once she's got the calculations, she's pretty ideal for being in there if an unforeseen element of the mission is altered." He points at the vault door being dismantled behind us. "Besides, she got it done. The others will have to start from scratch."

I turn to Jax. He nods in agreement.

AnneMarie huffs out an angry breath. "One more attempt." She glances at her display. "But you're already showing signs of fatigue and altered mental acuity from the repeated exposure to blasts."

I touch the tiny electrodes hidden in my pouffy updo. "I'm fine," I say. "I'll do it again."

And get it right. I hand my pack to a crew member, who passes me a fresh one. My ears are still ringing and I feel a little spacey, but I'm not giving up now.

"Reset the parameters," Jax says, making AnneMarie scowl harder. Normally that's her line. "Give her an all-new set of calculations."

"But we know the values in the vault," the Phase Two says.

"Give her a real challenge," Jax says.

Well, hell. I said I wanted to do this without his help, but I didn't exactly want him to make it *harder*.

Still, I don't say anything, shouldering the pack and checking the straps on the breakneck heels.

Jax doesn't even look my way, but strides back out the side door as if I'm any trainee. I wonder if he really does think I'm that good.

There's no reason to. I'm only here at all because of him. I would have lived out my life as a clueless civilian, except that fate threw us together. That's how I learned about this underground world.

Spies, mercenaries, high-tech surveillance. All watching the world so that the incompetent, the merciless, and the corrupt don't seize too much power.

It's where I want to be.

I just have to blow up this vault.

I head back down the hall to start the entire process over. My explosives trainer meets me at the rendezvous point. "You've got this," he says. His dark eyes peer into mine and his hands come up on either side of my forehead as if to squeeze more knowledge into me.

He's lean and strong, dark-skinned and half a head taller than me. "Shut out the internal warning systems that say you're injured or impaired," he says. "Hyper-focus on the task. She's gonna try and throw you on this one."

I nod. "Got it."

We wait together until my watch buzzes that the testing scenario is set and ready. Then I go.

The sequins on the bag dig into my arm as I hurry down the hall. I almost trip on the stupid shoes. Who wears crap like this? Since nobody will be around at this point of the mission anyway, I waste two of my precious seconds by slipping the straps off my heels and kicking them away. One less thing to waste mental energy on.

I turn the corner and approach the new door. Other than the lack of char marks, this one looks remarkably like the last one. But I'm not fooled. The explosives-training storage vault has hundreds of doors, every kind that can be manufactured. There is no telling what this one is like inside.

I press a device against the door, one that calculates the depth and provides a breakdown of the manufacturing materials.

But the display blinks off. I pull it away and tap it. It's gone dead.

So that's how they are going to play it.

I stick it in my pack and jerk a small ball-peen hammer from another pocket. I'll have to do this manually.

Doors have certain standards they follow for depth. I'll have to make an educated guess based on the specs I've memorized, overcompensate a bit, and keep my head during the blast.

Literally.

My ears are still ringing, but I tune it out.

The watch buzzes. Ninety seconds.

I tap the door and listen to the ringing sound it

makes. I tap several other spots. Thicker than the last one. It has a smaller internal opening for the mechanism. Harder to blow.

I stick another cylinder on the door. AnneMarie thinks I can't handle another blast, so she chose a door that needed more explosive power. This is as much about her as the mission itself. She expects me to fail.

I initiate the sequence and step back. The medical trainer who helped us learn to work through pain or panic or injury told me that in the case of a concussion or other debilitating head or inner-ear injury, I should give my brain an easy task to keep my amygdala calm. So I duck behind the concrete planter, turn my head to protect the already-pulsing ear, and picture my favorite knots. Bowline. Stopper. Clove hitch.

The loops and turns have precision, balance, and order. I tie them in my mind, breathing easy, waiting.

BOOM.

I turn into the blast and move with the shock wave. I'm thrown against the wall again, but this time, my shoulder hits first and my head doesn't connect to the wall.

I dash for the vault. The false ceiling is falling everywhere in chunks. I dodge a two-by-four, waving away dust.

The silver door has a ragged gaping breech. It's not enough for someone to see inside at a glance. I have to actually get it open.

I snatch my heat-shielding cloth and grasp the twisted handle. At first it doesn't give, but with a groan, the door eases wide.

At the training facility, there is nothing behind it but a steel-reinforced concrete wall. On the real mission, there will be an entire counterfeiting operation.

But what matters right now is that I did it.

2

JAX

Satisfaction swells in me as Mia's explosive charge tears a chunk out of the test door. And relief. I've known that Mia has great potential as a Vigilante. Everything I've seen of her since I kidnapped her at a safe house, thinking she had killed my partner, has told me she would be an asset to the network.

Not to mention, the Vigilantes are in her blood. Literally. Her parents were both operatives. And once we got some of her records freed, we confirmed that she is the last surviving family of

Prescott Adams, the original Vigilante first hired by President Eisenhower to establish this underground network.

But her recent struggles training for her qualifying mission have been difficult to watch. This is not entirely on her, of course. AnneMarie's training prowess did not exactly wow me. But something else has been at play. Something that seemed to distract her at the worst possible moment.

Like today.

I hope it isn't me.

I finger the ring box I keep in my pocket most of the time. Mia wants to prove herself. I can respect that. When I met her a year ago, she had lost everything. Her last family member. Her confidence. Tagging along with me had cost her even more — her home had been destroyed. Her safety compromised. And her innocence.

At first I'd kept her with me because I didn't know what else to do with her.

But now I know everything she can be.

I pull my hand away from the box and grasp the back of an empty chair next to AnneMarie, who is busily tapping her screen with notes.

Mia's voice floats over the speaker as she relays

14

the codes indicating that she has successfully opened the vault and the mission can proceed. She sounds professional and calm, if a bit giddy.

I turn to AnneMarie. "Success. She'll do fine."

AnneMarie glares at the screen. "It took her seven attempts. Not inspiring a high level of confidence."

I push the flare of anger down and keep my voice level. "You disarmed her tools, yet she succeeded anyway. And at a heightened level of difficulty. Far more than any of the other trainees have accomplished."

The tech nods in agreement. "We don't usually disable the diagnostics until Phase Four."

AnneMarie watches Mia in a monitor, her lips tight. I can see a small vein in her neck throbbing. Her anger amuses me. She's been riding Mia hard these past few months. I would do the same, but only because I know Mia can handle it. AnneMarie seems to do it because she enjoys it.

Now, however, she knows Mia is the best choice for this mission. No room for argument. "Fine," she says. She jabs a button and the wall slides open again.

Mia turns and stands at attention. Her face glows

with satisfaction.

"Well done, Ms. Morrow," says AnneMarie with only a hint of disappointment. "Despite your current reduced faculties, you successfully completed the training module. You are dismissed. Go to debriefing, then on to medical."

Mia smiles. "So does that mean I'm on the mission?"

"That is apparently now up to Mr. De Luca," AnneMarie says. Ice drips from her words.

I give Mia a nod. Mia's smile broadens.

"Yes, sir, thank you, sir!" she says, then turns and heads down the hall.

"Her blood is on your hands now, Mr. De Luca." AnneMarie's voice is still cold. "From what I hear, your antics give her plenty of opportunities to die."

I tug on my sleeves. "And her performance will be a reflection of your training. Prepare for an audit of your trainees' service records."

AnneMarie stiffens. I nod and let myself out of the control room.

Mia and I are generally careful about being too outward with our relationship while on duty. But as soon as I am out of the training bunkers and in the main hall, she pops through the open door of the debriefing room and jumps straight into my arms.

I hang on to her, relishing the feel of her body against mine, legs wrapped around my waist. I don't kiss her, though. No use getting that started. Silos are heavily monitored and recorded. We'd be giving the security techs a show.

"You're still barefoot," I murmur in her ear.

She laughs. "I despise spike heels."

"But you'll do anything for the mission."

She lowers her legs back to the ground. Without shoes, she is especially small, barely reaching my chest. I want to press a kiss into that honey-brown hair, even as trussed up as it is with hairspray, but I resist.

She squeezes my neck. "I almost wonder if you put me up for this one just to see me totter around in elegant shoes."

God, I'm already counting the hours until I can get her home. "Guilty. I assume you haven't seen medical yet."

"I'm headed there now." She lets go of me and presses a hand to her forehead. "I do have a killer headache."

"Seven blasts. Two today," I say. "That's a lot of hits to take."

She waves at the debriefing officer, and we head down the hall. When Mia completed her Phase One training and was being processed for her qualifying mission, I ensured she got the silo with the best health record.

I knew she would push herself to the point of injury. She was determined and hardheaded. I couldn't always keep her safe, but I could make sure that whoever was patching her up was the best.

We get to the stairwell. We have eight floors to ascend. "You up for the walk?" I ask. "We can call a medic trolley."

"No way," Mia says. "I'm too pumped to be rolled behind the walls."

"I'm willing to get on an elevator just for you."

She smiles as she opens the door. "Now that's devotion, Operative De Luca. I know how you hate them."

She does seem perky as she hurries up the flights. We arrive at our floor and come out on the landing that overlooks the main hub of the silo.

She sighs as she looks down. "This view never gets old."

Below, Vigilantes in every phase bear colors of each specialty, from driving to security to combat.

They wander among dozens of eight-foot glass monitors. Information specialists sort through data as it arrives, sending it where it belongs, from mundane cell-phone messages about cheating spouses to intercepted transmissions between guerrilla-warfare squads.

Here in the Washington silo, we don't just monitor our immediate area, but all incoming data from the United Nations, US government buildings, and foreign ambassadors living in the area. It's one of the largest and busiest silos in the world.

But I'm not particularly thrilled to be running it.

"Aren't you glad you came out of retirement?" Mia says, gesturing to the busy spectacle below. "You could be missing all this!"

I break protocol and tuck her hand inside my elbow. I hadn't missed this, not when I was alone with her in Switzerland, just us and the Alps and a cottage and her attempts to grow watermelon in Swiss soil. But I don't say so. This part of our lives is for her.

"Of course," I say. "It's your time to shine."

She beams, eyes alighting on the bustle below. "This is the most amazing life I could have imagined."

I pat her arm and let her go. "I believe you are expected at medical," I say.

"Yes, yes," she says. She gives her head a quick shake. "I will be glad to get rid of this persistent ringing."

We move toward the medical wing. "The protective tech didn't help?"

She pulls a small flesh-colored device from her ear. "I'm sure it did. Maybe it's not meant for as many blasts as I had to do."

I take it from her and examine it for damage. I'm a Phase Ten in three specialties, but medical tech isn't one of them. "I'll have it checked," I tell her.

We cross the busy hub and arrive at the hall leading to the medical wing.

The crisp, purified air here always makes me feel more alert. Mia seems to perk up from it as well, practically skipping as she approaches the checkpoint.

"Hello, Operative Morrow," a young man says. "We've been expecting you. Head back to Bay Four. Dr. James wants to check that inner ear."

"Have them test this as well," I say, passing him the device.

"You don't have to babysit me," Mia says to me. "I'm sure they're looking for you upstairs."

"I'm a pencil pusher now." I lean close to her ear. "Besides, there might be nudity involved back there."

She laughs and pushes against me. "Away with you, sir." She frowns when her hand lands on the bulge of the ring box. Her eyes dart down to my pocket, and her voice is a little shakier when she says, "We'll catch up later, okay, Jax?"

I step back with a curt nod. "Anything for you."

Mia gives me an uncertain smile as she moves toward the sliding doors. When they have closed behind her, I relax my tightened fists. I should stop being so sentimental. Mia wants to be a Vigilante, with all the danger and short-term thinking that the lifestyle entails. I have to respect it. It was a life I once loved too.

The halls are whisper silent. A Phase Four data specialist passes me and nods in quiet deference. I nod back. Those of us in suits rather than phase gear are always intimidating. I'm tired of it, frankly, but this is where I need to be for Mia.

So I should go all in. Don't hold back. Do the job like all these people deserve me to.

I spot a small door in the wall and approach it. When I pause, a green light activates. I wait as it scans me.

"Operative Jax De Luca," the confirmation voice says. The door slides open and a metallic ball rolls out. I press my palm to the hatch and wait for it to hiss open. Then I pull the engagement-ring box out of my pocket and drop it into the compartment.

"Awaiting instructions," the voice says.

"Put it in deep storage," I tell it. "No immediate access."

The ball closes and rolls back into the wall.

Done.

3

MIA

Jax decides to personally oversee my drop-off at the location of the mission. At first I want to tell him to let me do this on my own. But as the cloaked van approaches the office building that conceals the vault, my stomach starts flipping.

So I'm glad he's here.

"Just stay focused," Jax says. His voice is hard, all business, like I'm any trainee trying to earn Vigilante status.

I appreciate this. It's no time to be mushy. I wonder if he's still carrying the ring box. He knows

23

I asked him to wait until I tried the Vigilante life.

Maybe he hopes that if I fail, I will come back to his proposal.

My stomach quakes but I say, "It's a qualifying mission. You did yours at age twelve."

"All I had to do was con a couple kids."

"The good ol' days," I say. "Now we whippersnappers blow up counterfeiting rings."

"Be safe," he says, his voice serious now.

"As safe as I can be with a blast potential that could pop the top off a mountain." I sound much more confident than I feel, but I can tell it helps Jax. For someone like him, it's probably much harder to send someone off on a mission than to do it himself.

We approach a Vigilante car that is outfitted exactly like the girlfriend's white 2019 Mustang, right down to the dent in the side it got a year ago. I've been reading the girl's social media to get a feel for her. Her daddy bought her the car when she graduated high school two years ago.

"See you on the other side," Jax says. He almost leans in for a kiss, then catches himself.

I take the sequined sack purse from Fisk, the mission commander. I nod at them both, wait for the back door to slide open, then step down onto the

24

pavement in the ankle-breaking shoes. We're behind an abandoned strip mall just outside D.C. It's less than a mile from the vault.

A man in black steps out of the Mustang and walks away without a greeting. I slide into the seat and set my bag on the passenger side. The car might look like a civilian vehicle, but inside it's all Vigilante. If for some reason I'm unable to escape the mission undetected, the car will drive itself back to the van.

When I close the door, the dash voice says, "Operative Morrow identified for Mission VQ-2048. All cloaking deactivated. Civilian driving mode initiated." The car drops into a lower gear and the rumble of the engine gets louder and rougher.

I glance back at the van, but of course I can't see it. All its cloaking is on. If Jax is watching, I won't know.

Time to do this.

The drive to the office building is short. My dash screen shows the position of the other Vigilantes. They should be completing their elements of the mission — dropping in a looped video for surveillance and disabling the door alarms. That part is easy since the Vigilantes own almost all the companies that make security equipment. Everything, from electronic locks to retina scans, has a built-in Vigilante hack.

I've watched a half-dozen videos of the girlfriend to learn her mannerisms. I'm not supposed to talk if I can help it, but I've practiced a few things in case I have to.

Her name is Loretta, and she always visits around this time on Thursdays after getting her nails done. Tonight, though, she is off with girlfriends, so we're taking advantage of the disruption of her schedule to fool the other guards.

I glance down at my star-spangled fingernails as I turn the steering wheel. The things I do in the line of duty.

The Mustang pulls up to the side door of the office building. Like most illegal operations, this one has a front business. Avistor Solutions hires temporary office workers, although an examination of their books showed only four employees who have never been sent out.

There are three entrances to the building. The glass front. The delivery back. And this side door to the employee lot. Loretta always parks here.

The evening air is cool on my face as I get out of

the car and retrieve my bag. I tried to talk the supervisor out of the shoes, but they insisted these were Loretta's trademark. The guard at the security desk always makes a point of leaning over and checking them out. It is a fetish that Loretta enjoys and plays up to.

And essential to not blow the mission before it even begins.

I slip on a pair of oversized fashion glasses with a pink tint and walk up to the door. It's locked, of course, and I wave up at the video camera pointed down from the exterior wall. After a second, the latch pops.

So far, so good.

Just inside the door is the first security guard and a pair of screens that flip through views of the doors and hallways. Neither of them show the vault, of course, as we're still in the false front of the business. This guard has no idea.

"Loretta!" the man says. "Killer specs! Whatcha got on those toes today?" He stands and leans over the counter to take in my shoes. He whistles. "The Louboutins. Ace is treating you right."

I nod and twist a loose bit of hair. I watch his monitor until I see it click onto the hall I'm headed to. I press the timer on my watch, then I give him a little fluttery finger wave, same as I've seen Loretta do in videos.

I walk past him to a corridor on the right. I have to keep on her usual path until I get to the secondary security, the ones hired to watch the vault. No one can realize I'm not headed to the break room to wait on Ace to escort me down.

I pop into the women's bathroom as if I'm making a quick stop. I watch the seconds count to ten, know that the feed on the security desk has clicked away from this view, and hurry out. I rush to the stair door, stick a clear, thin cellophane-like device on it, push a button, and with a POP, the door unlocks. I hold my breath, but no alarm sounds. The Vigilantes are good.

I jerk the device off and stuff it in my bra. I'm inside, and the door is closed before the camera view can come back around.

The stairs are pitch black. I press one of the rhinestones on the glasses to flip on night vision. Ahead is the door to the other security station, the real deal.

I keep my count in my head. Ace walks by this station roughly every five minutes. I have to make it look like I'm with him, without him actually spotting me, as we pass the second desk. He'll obviously blow my cover if we engage, but the others should believe what they usually see.

I pull the thin device from my bra and pop the lock on the second door. I open it just a fraction as I tuck the device away again. The man by this set of monitors has his back to me. I watch the vault footage. I can't tell from this distance if it has the artifact that will prove it is in the loop. I'll check it as I pass.

Ace comes around the corner. He's stocky and good-looking, burred hair and an unshaven face. I wait for him to go by. The guard at the screens waves, then returns to the display.

I open the door and move quickly behind him. The guard turns again, sees me, and I point at Ace. He nods.

I stare at his screen as we walk. The small green pixel shows in the corner.

We're on.

I slow down, allowing Ace to turn left down the corridor ahead of me. Then I break right, pop the door in the opposite hall, and hurry to the stairs.

This goes down to the vault level.

I descend in the greenish night-vision light. I pop the last door and I'm in familiar territory, the hallway that the Vigilantes reconstructed for my tests. I no longer have to worry about the security cameras due to the loop, but I have two deadlines. The guard path on this level is shorter and he will pass every three minutes. I have to find out where he is and give myself the longest possible time frame to blow the vault.

I'm not supposed to take out any guards. That's not the point of this mission. The night shift doesn't even know what they are guarding, and Vigilantes leave the innocent alone.

My second deadline is with Ace. He will pass the security station again in five minutes without me, and the guard might ask where Loretta has gone. If I haven't blown the vault by then, they might find me in progress. I have basic combat training, but fending off a group of guards is not part of my current skill set.

My objective is to blow the vault, verify that it is open and visible, set three small fires, and get out. When the firefighters come, they'll find the operation and law enforcement can handle it from there. We're just here to expose it. Most people have no idea how often a supposed big bust by the cops was actually aided invisibly by the Vigilantes. But traditional law enforcement can't know that we exist.

That's where I come in.

There are two offices at this level, and both should be empty. If I am seen by the guard, I'll play the clueless girlfriend, but it's risky. I really need to spot him unseen to avoid a complication.

I arrive at the first door. There's no light beneath and it's unlocked. I slip inside to wait for the guard to pass. I double-check my pack and the backup fire canister tucked under my short skirt.

Then I give my watch two quick taps to let the Vigilantes know I'm safely downstairs. A double buzz against my skin lets me know they registered my response.

I hear footsteps on the tile. The guard passes. I click my watch to start my timer, wait for him to turn, and then head to the vault.

It's go time.

I jerk my pack around and snatch the device that will verify the depth of the door. The steel wall looms inside the narrow corridor. I look around, making sure my space is the same.

But it's not.

The concrete planter that was in the corner during the tests is missing. The protection I expected to have during the blast is gone. I'll be exposed.

My watch buzzes with the ninety-second warning.

Damn. I have to move forward.

I affix the device and get the readings. It's all as expected. They got that much right.

I grab the green cylinder and confirm the calculations. Maybe I can make a run for it and then circle back for the visual. If I make it to the turn in the hall, it will be fine. Just an increased risk of discovery if the guard is close and arrives before I'm gone.

It's a manageable risk.

The sticky strip comes clean and I press the explosive to the door. I look at the distance to the corner. Do I have time to lose the shoes or should I run in them? Which would be slower?

Both are slow. I might not even make it.

I could add time to the delay, but that increases the risk of discovery.

Which decision?

Delay. I'll delay it.

I override the presets, alter the sequence, and jerk the device away. I don't stop to take off the shoes. I just sprint.

But before I'm three steps away, the room shakes with a BOOM.

I'm thrown forward and crash into the wall. Metal and concrete and plaster rain down. It's too much. Way too much. My ears ring. A thousand shards of pain come over me.

I can't see anything. Everything has come down, the walls, the ceiling. But I'm alive. I'm thinking.

Thinking that no way should my blast have done that.

The damage is too great. And it blew too quickly.

My world is silent other than a ringing buzz. I can feel my chest heaving, trying to get some sort of breath in the dust and smoke. I reach for the bag but it's been blown from my shoulder. I feel the stickiness of blood on my arm and a fiery burning sensation at my waist.

I have to crawl through the wreckage, my knees and hands spiking with pain as they land on debris. I have no idea where I am, where the corner is, how to get back to the door. Through the dust I can see the pulsing red light of an alarm. Probably there's a sound too, but I can't hear it. My head only registers the ringing of my ears in the silence.

I'm far enough away now that I can stand. I stumble in the shoes but I'm grateful for them. I don't want to walk barefoot through this.

I tap my Vigilante watch two times to signal I'm alive, then three more to signal the mission is off course.

I keep moving forward. The guard should not have been affected by the blast. Hopefully he'll move away from it, not toward it. I'm behind schedule. I could run into him.

My watch buzzes a code, a request to communicate. I tap out a no and plod forward.

Mercifully, I find the door to the stairs. I careen up them, trying to decide my course of action.

Without my bag, I can't set three fires as planned, but one well-placed one will be enough.

Sounds start to intrude. The distant wail of a fire alarm. At least my ears aren't permanently damaged. I push the pain away from the other injuries. They can't be too bad if I'm still moving.

I skip the second level, the secure one with Ace

and the guard station, and get back to the ground floor. I dive into the bathroom and pull the spare fire canister out from under my skirt.

There's a small closet in the bathroom, and I jerk it open, hoping to find cleaning supplies. I shove aside the nonflammable scrubbing products and sure enough, there's an industrial-sized bottle of carpet cleaner.

I kick open several cases of toilet paper and spread them all around, dousing them with carpet cleaner. I have to make sure somebody reports the fire, or that vault downstairs will never be discovered. You can't even tell on this level that anything has happened down below.

The guards near the vault will be instructed not to call for help. But a fire up here will get reported by the outside. Someone will drive by and see it. Or the houses up the road will dial 911. I was supposed to set three, but one will have to do.

I spot a trash can and get another idea. Risky, but ensures the mission's success.

I dump loose paper towels into it along with the carpet-cleaner bottle. I move it close to the door. This is ridiculous, but I'm going to do it.

I take the fire canister and open it wide. The

exposure to oxygen sets it aflame. I have twenty seconds to get away from it before it bursts wide. I light a roll of toilet paper and dump it in the trash can. Then I toss the canister onto the line of drenched rolls.

The can rumbles as I push it to the other end of the hall. I hear the security guard's "Hey — Loretta? Is that you?" right as the bathroom door bursts open in flames.

I hightail it down the hall, shoulder-smack an office door, and force my way in. I turn to lock it in case the guard is crazy enough to follow me through the fire, and dump the trash can over on a pile of paper. It swiftly ignites.

The overhead sprinklers pop open, but only the tiniest trickle comes out. The water's off for the moment. Perfect. The mission is on track, even though I had to improvise. I turn to the window.

It doesn't open, so I swing an office chair through it, sending shards of glass into the bushes below. This isn't the elegant exit I was supposed to execute, but then, I didn't leave three neat canister fires behind me either.

The heels sink into the soft ground. In the distance, I can already hear the wail of sirens. Yes.

The fire department will come, douse the small fires, discover the counterfeiting operation down below, and my mission will be done.

After a quick command on my watch, the Mustang pulls right up to me. I swing inside and dart away at Vigilante speed just as the orange flames shoot out the bathroom window.

The bad guys are getting caught today.

4

JAX

Unbelievable.

The visual on the office building where Mia is working looks right, but everything that calculated the blast below has gone red.

"The car has registered Operative Morrow at the wheel," a man says. "She's headed for the rendezvous point."

I let out a long exhale. "What's the status of the vault?" I ask.

"Unknown, sir," he says. "Extensive damage. We've commandeered the video, but it's all dust and debris. Morrow denied a voice hail. You want someone to go in for a visual?"

"Ask Fisk," I say. "I'm just dead weight on this gig."

The communications specialist grins at me.

Fisk himself spins in his chair. "I'll await Morrow's report. She was there. They'll be on full alert at the vault now. No use compromising the mission at this point." He runs his hand across his flattop, thinning above his forehead. "What were the parameters on the blow?"

The specialist reviews the data. "Blast volume twenty percent over expected conditions. Blast delay seven seconds under recommended detonation lead time."

"What the hell was she thinking?" Fisk says. "What made her increase the blast and shorten the delay?"

"Something about the situation, sir," the com specialist answers. "We'll have to ask her."

Fisk turns back to his monitor. "Head to rendezvous."

I force myself calm and silent. If Mia changed the blast, she had her reasons. I know it.

"She's going to need a medic," the com

specialist adds. "The vehicle reports decreased lung capacity, increased respiration, and blood loss."

Now I can't stay silent. "Get on that," I hiss. "Send a helicopter to rendezvous."

Fisk whirls his chair. "I don't see any need to dispatch anything that visible. We can have a medic there inside six minutes." His mouth quirks. "We'll take care of her. Don't worry about that."

I sit back, angry at myself for interfering. Mia would be fine. She was tough. She'd obviously completed the mission and set the fires after the blast. She wasn't dying.

The van raced down the highway. "Three minutes to intercept," the com specialist says. "And we're only seeing one set of fire-canister data, the backup device."

Fisk nods. "Lost the others in the blast, no doubt. Does GPS still show them at the site?"

The com specialist taps calmly on his monitor. "Yes."

"Destroy them remotely," Fisk says.

More taps. "Done. Fire department arriving on the scene," he says.

Fisk returns to his own screen. "All good. Might have been messy, but looks like it went off."

I want to say, "Of course it did," but I've done enough talking already. Ahead, we arrive at the rendezvous, a car body shop on the Vigilante books. The farthest bay door is rolled up and the white Mustang is inside.

I still can't relax. Not until I see her.

A second bay door rolls up as we approach. When we're in, both doors come down. I force myself to sit still. Fisk doesn't need me breathing down his neck while she debriefs him. He heads out for the initial report.

I watch out the side window as the Mustang opens and Mia emerges. When I see how covered in blood she is, there's no way I'm staying inside. I'm out of the van before the com guy can even look up.

Mia holds out an arm when she sees me. "I look bad, Jax, but I'm okay. It's mostly superficial." She's breathing heavily, with pauses between words.

"The blast was high," Fisk says.

"That's not how I set it," Mia says. "And I added time, not took it away. The concrete planter—" She stops to cough.

I take another step toward her, but she waves me off again. After a moment, she is able to keep going.

"The concrete planter was gone. I had no shield, so I added a delay to make a run to the corner."

"But it blew early," Fisk says.

"Yeah, it nailed me."

The third bay opens and a medic van outfitted like a traditional ambulance pulls in. Two women jump out, holding red duffel bags.

I move aside as they rush up, instantly putting an oxygen mask on Mia's face and scanning her for wounds and internal injuries.

"We remotely destroyed the fire canisters," Fisk says. "I assume the bag got blown off you during the blast."

Mia nods, watching the medics assess her. One turns to Fisk. "We should get her to the silo," she says. "Lots of contusions here and she has a piece of steel embedded in her side."

Mia's voice is muffled as she says, "Really?" She lifts her arm and looks down, but the fluttery bits of the torn shirt make it hard to see anything but streaks of dirt and blood.

"She could go into shock," the medic says. "You want a stretcher?"

Mia shakes her head. The three of them walk toward the third bay.

"I assume you're going with her," Fisk asks.

Every instinct in me is screaming that I should follow them. But Mia has already pushed me away twice. I'm going to obey her.

And I want to know why there is a discrepancy between what Mia plugged into the device and what actually happened.

"I'll go see her at medical," I tell Fisk. We walk to the van as the medics help Mia into the back of the ambulance. "What would account for the error in the device? It could have killed her."

Fisk climbs into the van. "We'll go over the logs for who assembled, tested, and double-checked the blast equipment," he says. "But generally there is only one accounting for why something like this happens — operator error."

I want to punch him, but I quell my rage. I sit in my chair, crossing one leg over the other. I'm glad for the suit, the impeccable fit. I feel calmer and in control as I turn to him. He's in steel-gray Phase Six commander gear. Not a high-level Vigilante, but then, a qualifier mission generally doesn't need one.

"So you believe Mia entered the wrong blast parameters, even though she's been fully tested? And she reduced the blast delay rather than

43

increasing it, even though that is easily a fatal mistake?"

Fisk shrugs. "She's a Phase One and didn't do that hot in the training pod. I wouldn't have put her in a job like this."

Now I have to forcibly clench the armrests to avoid incapacitating his idiotic, mind-numbing stupidity. "Operative Morrow has managed situations far more difficult than this with accuracy and ingenuity. I don't believe for a minute that she entered the wrong data."

Fisk seems to realize he's pissing off a superior. "Like I said, we'll go over the logs." He turns to stare me down. "I think your objectivity on this mission is compromised. I respect the hell out of you," he says, "but I think when it comes to Mia, you'd best back the hell off."

I've had enough. I flick my wrist and code my watch to take over the vehicle, a perk of being head of syndicate. Any vehicle can be mine.

The van comes to a dead halt in the middle of the highway. "To the medical facility, auto-drive, top speed," I say into the watch face. The van abruptly turns around and heads the other direction.

Fisk whirls away in annoyance.

I'm not going to believe that Mia made a mistake. If she says she did it right, I'm going to back her up, no matter what. These clowns can check their data. I know firsthand that the Vigilante network isn't foolproof.

But despite how angry I am at Fisk, I have to acknowledge one thing.

I'm definitely not objective.

5

MIA

The medic peels the bandage away to apply a fresh one. He's a different one from yesterday, when I was brought in. He likes to tell gory jokes.

"You're going to have a nice Vigilante badge of honor here," he says.

I dare to take a peek. A raw, jagged line glistens with some sort of medical superglue that will supposedly heal faster. "I guess I can go as a new-age Bride of Frankenstein for Halloween," I say.

He laughs. "I was just teasing. If I do my job right, you won't even scar."

I wince as he presses the new pad against my skin. "Do all Vigilantes have things like this happen on their qualifying mission?" I ask.

"Only the lucky ones," he says, stepping back to survey his work. "Most get some mundane tech or surveillance gig."

Lucky. Sure. Getting blown half to bits was lucky.

Mission Commander Fisk enters the medic bay. "How is Operative Morrow?" he asks.

The medic closes my gown and whisks away the wrappers from the bandage, all business now. "Surgical removal of shrapnel went perfectly. Lungs cleared during the night. No infections present at this time on the wounds. We're sending her home."

Fisk nods curtly. "Thank you." He waits for the young man to leave the bay and approaches the end of the bed.

I feel strange in my hospital getup in front of the commander. "Everything okay?" I ask.

"I'm glad you're well," he says. "Unfortunately, the counterfeiting equipment was buried in the rubble badly enough that the firefighters did not investigate it. By the time any adjustors or inspectors get in there, the operation will be dismantled or destroyed. They'll set up elsewhere."

I sit up despite the ripping pain. "What? So it was a failure?"

"It's been bumped upstairs. They'll send higher-level Vigilantes on their trail now. We'll get them anyway. It's just no longer a job for a Phase One."

Oh my God. I'd blown it. Despite everything, I'd failed.

I force my voice steady as I ask, "So what happens to me now?"

"We're awaiting your orders. That will be up to your training director." His expression is stony and impassive. "You kept your head in there, Morrow. Most wouldn't have continued the mission after a blast like that."

"Did anybody figure out why it went off early?"

His face flickers for a second, but his voice is unchanged as he says, "The device went off based on the parameters that were set."

"But...I delayed it. And I didn't change the blast volume."

"The settings were altered on the device. It was a high-pressure situation outside your training," he says. "Could've happened to anybody."

But not a Vigilante, I think. I'd screwed up

somehow. I hadn't kept my head at all. I'd nearly lost it.

"It was a pleasure doing a mission with you. Good luck," Fisk says. And with a quick spin, he heads out.

God. Now what? Am I out? What happens to Phase Ones who fail their qualifiers?

Now that I am alone, tears threaten. But every room is monitored, and I can't let them see that. For all I know, they are watching to see how I handle the news to determine my fate.

I shift so my legs hang off the edge of the bed and jump off. The reverberation sends a million shards of pain through my body, but I don't let it show on my face. I pick up my Vigilante watch from its pod on a table by the wall. I bring up the screen and request a meeting with AnneMarie so that I can be given my next directive.

I absolutely plan to report for duty despite my medical leave. I won't take pain meds. I won't take a day off. They are going to see how tough I am. Maybe I'm not meant to calculate blast volume. But there is a place for me here. I know it.

Modesty is pointless in a silo with all the surveillance, so I just drop the gown and reach for the Phase One Trainee jumpsuit that has been waiting in a bag on the chair.

Jax's voice rumbles behind me. "I knew there would be nudity back here," he says.

I jump and turn, the package against my chest. "I need to control my startle reflex," I say.

He strides toward me, crossing the bay in three long steps. "You're looking better."

I glance down at my exposed skin, nicks and cuts and bruises covering my side and back. "It's not as bad as it could be," I say.

He pulls me in. His suit is silky and cool. I flatten my cheek against his lapel. He smells expensive, like wood chips and fine linen. I think back to the Swiss Alps, when he'd given up the suits for casual wear, shorts and T-shirts with funny sayings. He'd been so different. His body had relaxed, not so rigid and tight. Now he was practically in fight stance, ready for anything.

Maybe I'd been wrong to bring us back here.

He moves the bag away and picks up a soft robe from the bottom of the bed. He wraps me in it. I take a moment to just be held and protected, not the badass Vigilante, but Jax's girl.

Is this better? Is this what I should be instead?

"I believe in you," he says quietly, his breath ruffling my hair. "I know you set that blast correctly. I don't buy for a minute that the mistake was yours."

I can't look up at him. "I might have been under too much pressure. I did override the presets."

"And set them to a more favorable parameter. Even a first grader knows ten seconds is longer than three."

I wince inside. It was such a terrible mistake. And it had cost me. And the network. And AnneMarie. And Fisk.

And Jax. He'd stuck his neck out for me.

And I'd failed.

"I asked to meet with AnneMarie," I say.

I feel the push of his chest as he huffs his annoyance at her name. "She's going to be all self-righteous."

My eyes prick again, but I shove the emotion down. "She was right. I wasn't ready for the job."

Jax grasps my arms firmly and sets me far enough away from him that he can see me. "Mia, that mission was tough."

"What would you have done?" I ask. "You're a Phase Ten. How would you have done it?"

"I would have done exactly what you did. Reset the parameters to ensure I got a visual."

"But you wouldn't have screwed it up."

He lifts me to sit on the bed, the soft robe swallowing me. His eyes hold my gaze with searing intensity. "I'm going with the assumption you did not screw it up. If I couldn't get a visual quickly, the only thing to do would be to get out and draw the fire anyway, just as you did. You did exactly what I would have done."

I drop my chin. "But it wasn't good enough."

"The only problem with this mission was that it was a qualifier. For any other mission, we would just be going back and finding another way in."

I try to keep my voice steady. "But since it was, I didn't qualify."

He doesn't answer. The pod is deathly quiet, protected from outside sounds. Nothing even beeps or hums. It's like we're nowhere. I'm nowhere. Going nowhere.

"I'll see what I can do," Jax says.

"No," I answer quickly. "If I'm out, it's because I should be out."

Silence falls again.

Jax reaches out and rubs his thumb across the

back of my hand. My breathing slows and the myriad pains and stings from the cuts and bruises ease a notch.

"Do you regret coming back here?" I ask. My voice is small, like a child's.

He draws me back against him. "Of course not. This time of our lives is for you."

I turn my face into his chest. Maybe this was what was meant to happen. I wouldn't regret trying. I had given it everything I had.

My watch beeps. I turn my head and glance down at it. It's a message from AnneMarie's scheduler.

I'm to see her immediately.

6

JAX

After I leave Mia for her meeting with her training director, I head out of the silo. I want to have a conversation away from the Vigilante network, and I can't do that easily inside. As head of syndicate, I'm given the privilege of a secure communications room, which allegedly isn't monitored or recorded.

But I'm not one to trust anybody. There is always someone trying to work every system.

I drive my Aston Martin out of the secure holding facility in full cloak mode as I speed away from the silo and across the plains.

I don't follow a road, but cut through the weedy grassland. If anyone looked at the car, they might see occasional glints of light, the spin of a tire that feels like a mirage, and the whip of the random stalks of wheat as the car's movement blows them aside.

Cars cannot fully cloak in daylight, but it's close. The exterior will mimic the surroundings. It's enough that Vigilante drivers in training aren't allowed to use it until they are well trained in evasive maneuvers. Civilians will drive right at you.

Eventually I come to a highway and take it at top speed for about twenty minutes, until I know I'm out of range of any moderated city surveillance. I pull onto a tiny side road and turn down a long drive heading into the trees. My screen says there is an unoccupied house at the end of it. The owners, the Fitzgeralds, are on a cruise. No crime data. No suspicious activity. Nothing in fifteen years to make it worth bothering to monitor.

So I stop.

I get out of the car, ditching my Vigilante watch and phone and all the tech on the driver's seat. Then I walk a while, taking in the tree branches swaying overhead and the undulating movements of the dead grasses of the Fitzgeralds' unused acreage.

When I sense that I'm as remote as I can be, I pull out a Blackphone my friend Sam made for me. It's composed of non-Vigilante parts and is as off grid as a device can be. Sam is a Phase Ten tech who's as brilliant with gadgets never conceived of before as he is with a hammer and a roll of baling wire. He's one of the few people I trust all the way to the bone.

I call him now.

His voice booms through the speaker. "Jax, boy! How is the big cheese doing up there in the land of pointless politics?"

"A kill order a day," I say. "You still peeved at the doughnut man for shorting you a bear claw? I can erase him."

Sam laughs. "Nah. He made it good."

There is silence for a moment and I know he's working to get himself off grid too. Then he says, "All right, we're cool now. What's going on?"

I look out across the field at a flock of barn swallows that rise in a spiral into the sky. It reminds me of Switzerland, and how we had the time to notice the flight of birds.

"Mia did her qualifying mission yesterday," I say. "The explosives she set went rogue. I'm convinced she calculated it right, but it blasted too hot and too fast. She was pretty injured."

"She okay?" Sam's voice is full of concern. He always did have a soft spot for Mia.

"She's all right. About to meet with Wash about her future in the network."

"Wash? Really? Bloody hell."

"That about sums it up," I say.

"Let me locate the device," Sam says.

"You in a secure place?"

"Close enough." He's quiet for a moment. I start walking again.

"I see three blasts yesterday. I assume hers was outside D.C.?"

"That would be the one."

A rabbit darts through the grass. I stop a few feet from it, admiring its graceful leaps.

It pauses a moment to look at me, as if trying to determine whether I'm a threat. I want to laugh. I could send out an order right now to take out any human on this planet inside of an hour, from a grocery sacker to a president. But I have no way to catch a rabbit.

He sits there, brown and white, furry and fat, eyes on me. "I'm nobody," I tell him.

"You got somebody with you?" Sam asks.

"Not a soul. In a field with a rabbit."

"So you're talking to bunnies now?"

"Politics will make you just that crazy."

"I hear ya," he says. "Okay, I'm going to take a deeper look later, but right now I'm seeing that that blast blew exactly the way it was programmed to do."

"Look at the change to the presets. See what was programmed in."

"That's what I'm doing, boss. Last-minute reset. Blast volume increased twenty percent. Time delay reduced by seven seconds."

I grip the phone tightly and look up into the sky. "How many sequence changes were needed to do that?"

"What do you mean?" Sam asks.

"How many keystrokes? What would be the difference between just changing the delay, and changing both the delay and the blast?" I look down again for the rabbit, but he's gone. I got too loud. Became a threat.

"I get where you're going with this, boss, but

when you go into the presets, everything opens up. If she bumped anything, she could have altered several parameters. It's designed to be accessed easily and changed rapidly. You can't just go stabbing at numbers."

I turn and start heading back to the car. "All right. Let me know if you figure anything else out."

"I don't think she'd screw up either," Sam says. "And I'm not saying she did. But it looks like it from here."

"Thanks, Sam."

I power down the phone. Ahead of me, the Fitzgeralds' homestead sits like a sentinel in its grassy field, a few trees giving it shade. Nobody for a half mile, easy.

I wasn't sure what Mia's fate was going to be. But maybe we could find a bit of Switzerland right here in D.C. The Fitzgeralds had.

I guess it was time to see what AnneMarie Wash would do with her.

7

MIA

I was sort of wishing I'd at least taken some ibuprofen as I stood in the pod outside AnneMarie's office, waiting for her to make time for me.

I had been waiting a little over an hour. A sheepish Phase Two information tech sitting at a glass monitor offered me some water. I turned it down. I would stand here with my pain. I would do whatever it took to impress her after my screwup.

A medic walks in. "Eat this or else," he says, passing me a squeeze pouch.

"Why?"

He lifts my arm and scans the implant under my skin that will monitor me for a week post-surgery. "Because this says you have low blood sugar, and you're trying to heal."

I *am* a little woozy. I twist the top of the pouch and squirt the pale yellow substance into my mouth. Applesauce spiked with some flavor. Raspberry, maybe.

"All of it," he says.

I scrunch the pouch until it is depleted and pass it back. "Happy?"

The door behind us slides open. "Getting a little snack?" AnneMarie says, her voice dripping with derision.

The medic turns to her. "Medical rations. She's only twenty hours post-op. Wasn't even discharged when she came down."

Her black eyes dart to me. "Did she leave against medical orders?"

Great. She was going to find the worst in everything, no matter what.

"Operative Morrow was not under any orders," the medic says. "She's been remarkably tough and resilient for what she's been through."

"You mean what happened due to her mistake."

AnneMarie's glossy black hair cuts across her forehead like an ax blade. She's sixty, easy, so her hair has a wig-like quality even though it's clearly her own. Not a hint of gray, either.

I'm not quite sure what to do. I haven't said a word and the two of them are talking as if I'm not right in front of them.

The tech at the desk stands up to get our attention. "You have six minutes until your next appointment," she says to AnneMarie.

"I won't keep you," the medic says and turns to me. "Stop by medical before leaving the silo. You'll need instructions about the bandage and any limitations on your activities."

"Yes, sir," I say. "Thank you."

AnneMarie whirls around to the door of her office. It slides open without a scan. When I approach, however, red lines cross the entrance. I wait as the scanner overhead identifies me. I'm not sure what would happen if I went through anyway. The hair-thin lines seem harmless, but for all I know they would singe me into oblivion.

When I enter, I see that AnneMarie's office overlooks part of the training pod. Below, five Phase Ones are doing combat obstacles. They duck beneath vehicles and shoot dart guns through walls of flame. I didn't do anything like that during my training. It wasn't my track.

AnneMarie watches the trainees for a moment, not so much as flinching when a young man's protective suit catches fire. It goes out in seconds, just long enough for the error to register in the logs. "He'll be excused from the program," she says. "He doesn't think swiftly enough on his feet for this type of operative."

"Where will he go?" I ask. It's definitely easier to talk about someone else's failure than my own.

"He'll work inside a silo. Since he failed his identified area of specialty, he'll be sent into tech and information." She turns away from the window. "We always need more of those, and not everyone is cut out to be a field agent with a ranking specialty."

I can only assume she is also talking about me. But explosives were not in my skill set. I take in a breath to say this but she holds up her hand.

"I don't know what to do with you. A special has no business in the Vigilante program."

This is the first time anyone has mentioned my status as a special. We're rare inside the network, a designation reserved for people whose actions and movements are not tracked, usually for our own protection.

The Vigilante network made me a special at the death of my parents because I was the last surviving descendent of Operative 001, Prescott Adams. I wasn't supposed to ever join the network, but Jax had accidentally dragged me in.

And I wanted more.

"My special status is not my choice," I say.

"But spreading your legs in all the right places is." Her voice has an edge.

I decide to accept the truth in her accusation that I slept with Jax to get inside the network. "I do what it takes," I say. "It's gotten me this far."

"Well, then." AnneMarie drops into her sleek black chair. "That's the first interesting thing you've said since we were introduced."

Might as well go for broke. I cross my arms in front of my white Phase One suit like I'm a tough girl, not a trainee scared to death about being kicked out. And I press on.

"I've talked my way out of a high-security silo and then into the most-guarded building in the nation. I can probably make you believe anything about me." I sound a heck of a lot more confident than I feel, but her dark eyebrow lifts anyway.

"That's well and good," she says, "but it doesn't change the fact that you failed your qualifying mission, left a mess for us to clean up, and now a case that should have been simple has been sent upstairs to level six."

"It wasn't a Phase One mission to begin with," I say. "It involved infiltration, impersonation, detonations, plus multiple objectives."

I've pushed too far, apparently, because AnneMarie spins around in her chair to look out the window again.

"Don't flatter yourself," she says. "Vigilantes with decades of experience determine the skill level of a mission, and the qualifiers always have layers. All you had to do was flash your legs, find a vault, and use a preset to blow it. Then drop three canisters on your way out."

She whips back around, her hair an unmoving, glossy black helmet. "And you blew it."

"Technically," I say, "I was supposed to."

"Don't be cheeky with me."

I drop my arms. The tough-girl bit isn't working. Vigilantes aren't like the military, where deference to higher ranks is required. But it seems like some humility might be in order.

"I apologize," I say. "The Vigilantes are just important to me. I do not wish to be dismissed."

She taps her desktop and a glass screen rises from the smoky gray surface. It blinks on with a scroll of data and images. She touches one of the boxes and a video of my training comes up.

"Just watch yourself," AnneMarie says. "And think of what you'd do in my position."

In the video, I shoot a dart gun at a target, once, twice, three times, until I hit the proper mark. The ammunitions instructor arrives and explains that the respiratory dart is best administered to the upper chest.

"It took you three rounds of training sequences to pass darts," AnneMarie says. She brings up my score card. "And your numbers were not impressive even then."

She pushes the video aside. "Look at a typical Phase One's dart record." We watch a few seconds of another young woman's race along a target practice, aiming a dart gun at six approaching targets and nailing the respiratory, neurological, and gastrointestinal darts in the correct locations with precision accuracy.

Her score card is the opposite of mine, all the Xs on the far end of the excellence line.

I want to point out that marksmanship was not part of my specialty and that I only had to master the basics, just like in combat and explosives. But I sense it doesn't matter. AnneMarie is playing with me like a cat who has trapped a mouse's tail. She's already decided my fate.

"So what happens to me now?" I ask. My voice is no longer bold or confident.

"We've found a good spot for you," AnneMarie says. "In archives. You'll increase the quality of the network's data by removing unnecessary input from the primary information core."

She sends the screen back down into her desk. "It's a critical position. I know I certainly don't want the system to process random garbage."

My stomach hits my toes. I feel like a CEO demoted to the mail room.

"What is the appeals process?" I ask over the lump in my throat that threatens to choke me.

AnneMarie laughs, an ugly, raspy sound. "Your appeal was used when your lover got you another chance on the training floor." She leans on the desk, her eyes like daggers. "You're done."

My Vigilante watch buzzes. I glance at the screen and see I have a notification of my new position in the network. So it really is set.

I don't have anything else to say to her, so I just turn and head for the door. This time I'm allowed to pass through without a scan.

Jax is here somewhere. He's probably found out the same as me, with a notification about my new position. I'm sure it went to everyone. My explosives trainer. The medics. The Phase One directors.

Humiliating.

I walk down the hall toward medical, feeling every ache from my injuries now that the adrenaline is dropping. Instead of taking the main corridor, I head to the secure hall where I'll encounter fewer people. I approach the scan door, but when the light passes over me, it goes red.

A voice says, "Operative Morrow does not have clearance for the secure hall. Please proceed to the main route."

"But I just used it this morning," I say to the door.

It doesn't respond. Even the machines don't have to answer to me anymore. Obviously archives is a huge step down.

But then I remember, I'm a special. I should have top clearance regardless.

I step away, then approach the door again. Before it can complete the scan, I tell it, "Special Mia Morrow."

The voice simply repeats, "Operative Morrow does not have clearance for the secure hall."

I have no choice but to turn around.

Apparently I'm worse off than when I started.

8

JAX

I message Mia as soon as I see her assignment has gone through. Jesus. Archives? This is the same level as manual labor, the cleaning staff and maintenance inside the silo. Those positions are generally given to family of Vigilantes who aren't interested in fieldwork or risk. Not everybody is.

Mia doesn't respond right away. I pace my office. I'm supposed to be reviewing a Phase Ten mission that is approaching, one involving the president, a prime minister, and two heads of state. But my head isn't in it.

It's on Mia.

I spot her on the other side of the glass, approaching my door at full tilt. But when the scanner hits her, it won't open. She doesn't have clearance for my own damn office.

I slam my fist on the override next to my screen and the door opens.

"I've lost my special status!" she says as she bursts in. "Not only am I in archives, I can't even do what I could before!" Her face contorts. "I screwed up, Jax. I shouldn't have tried. I wasn't raised Vigilante. I'm not cut out for this."

I walk around the desk to pull her into my arms.

"I'll get your special status corrected. Probably somebody in security didn't know what to do with you since you'd been demoted. There aren't a whole lot of specials to begin with, and certainly none going through training."

"What about Jovana?" she asks. "She was a special and a Vigilante."

My blood rises just hearing her name. Jovana betrayed me years ago, landing me in prison. Then she hounded Mia, kidnapping her at one point. She's been off grid again for over a year.

"She was a Vigilante first, and a special later," I

say. "And all that was for a purpose. It wasn't an organic designation."

"Is she still?" Mia asks. "A special?"

"Currently, yes," Jax says. "The committee does not have the power to act on an individual. Only on the system."

"Well, who does? Couldn't she just waltz in here? She has more clearance than I do!"

"No, she doesn't," Jax says. "We put a lock on her Vigilante status, and that will hold her out, special or not."

She's been breathing fast, but she starts to calm. "What will I be doing in archives?" she asks.

"You're not going there," I say. "I'm not going to have them bury you like that."

She looks up at me. "No, you can't do that. It's what I earned." She lets go of me and drops into a chair. "Unless I just quit entirely."

I think of the ring box in deep storage. "I'll support whatever you want to do," I tell her.

"Can I work my way up from archives?" she asks.

I hesitate. "It's never been done," I say. "I can't think of any field agents who came from tech after they'd been assigned." When her face falls, I add,

"But then, there's never been a special come into the program, either."

She gets up from the chair again and walks across the office. It's circular, like most silo rooms, and has a large oval conference table surrounded by chairs as well as my personal desk. She leans over and rests her head on the shiny tabletop.

I'm caught by the sight of her in the form-fitting white Phase One jumpsuit. If I've ever had a distraction and a weak spot, it's definitely her.

But I walk over and lay a hand on her back. "What would you like to do, Mia?" I ask. "I can make almost anything happen."

"Auto-eject AnneMarie from the silo," she says with a laugh. "I want to see her cartoon figure flailing as she flies across the plains."

This makes me smile. "I'm sure a catapult could be arranged. Not exactly new tech."

She lifts her head. "Jax, what do I do?"

I massage her shoulders. "Well, first, we'll get your secure status reinstated. And someone will get reprimanded for that mistake.

Then, I'll take you down to archives while we see what pathways there are for reassignment of your specialty and a new qualifying mission that is more appropriate for your skills."

Mia stands up and I wrap my arms around her. "You think my skill set wasn't correctly assigned?"

"You have a lot of talents," I say. "No reason why they can't be shifted to another area."

She leans her head back against my chest. "A lot of talents?"

My groin tightens. "I still haven't forgotten the first time you tied me to the seat of my car."

She closes her eyes. "I forced you to kiss me."

"You did." My fingers trail along her arm.

"I missed you last night," she says. "The pod was lonely."

"I put in a security override but that blasted surgeon stopped me from going in there personally."

Mia laughs lightly. "He knew better than to let you in."

"Did they tell you how long you had to wait?"

She turns around in my arms. "All they said was no strenuous lifting until I'm checked in a few days. The wound was pretty minor for a medical team like this."

"Nothing strenuous, then?" I lift her until she's seated on the table, her legs on either side of me.

"Can Jax be gentle?" She tilts her chin up.

I kiss her. I should keep my hands off her, I know it. But she's so tempting, so close. And I missed her last night.

I hold the back of her head and dive into her mouth. She tastes slightly sweet, like applesauce. Medical rations. I remember them from my own escapades. My hands graze her side and feel the bandage. I break the kiss.

"Too risky," I say, and let her go. "We should wait."

Her legs tighten around me. "You should have thought of that before you kissed me."

I glance up at the ceiling of the office, where invisible cameras monitor all the activity of the room. "We'll have witnesses," I warn her.

She tilts her head toward the opening of the secure pod. "But not in there?"

I haven't used the pod since taking over the position of head of syndicate. I don't buy into its security for high-risk conversations, but for this, maybe.

"All right," I say. I lift her from the table, her legs wrapped around my hips. I carry her as carefully as I can over to the pod. It scans me, hesitates when it encounters Mia as well, then the door slides silently open.

Inside is a cushioned oversized armchair, a small side table, and a communications box that stays silent and dark unless activated.

I kneel down and set Mia on the chair. "I think I can be non-strenuous," I say.

"I'm having my doubts about that," she teases.

I pull off her Phase One Trainee shoes and toss them outside the pod, since they contain a lot of data and tracking chips inside. Then I press the button to close the pod.

The silence is pure. I grasp the front zipper to Mia's jumpsuit and pull it down with measured slowness. She watches my hands, her breathing shallow.

I reveal the crisp white standard-issue bra. It's intended to protect her, so it's thick and sturdy, but I can still see the outline of Mia's tight nipples beneath it.

I slide the suit off her shoulders. Her head falls back on the chair. I take my time peeling it down, careful over the bandage, gentle over the nicks and bruises from the explosion.

The suit puddles at her waist, just above the band of her underwear, more standard equipment. I lift her hips to tug the jumpsuit farther down. The white panties fit trimly across her hips.

One leg, then the other, comes out of the pants. I toss the suit aside, enjoying the vision of Mia in the trainee undergarments on the dark red chair. I lift her hand and kiss the skinned knuckles, then make my way up her arm to the wide band of the bra. While my fingers slide it off her shoulder, I move up to her ear and kiss her hair. It smells different than usual, washed in the medical unit, smelling simple and clean rather than the lavender she favors at home.

I want to devour her but bide my time, exposing one breast and touching her tenderly. She sucks in a breath and I pause, but she nods, her head next to mine. "I'm all right," she whispers.

My lips find hers, then go lower, capturing the tight bud in my mouth. She sucks in again and her hips rise against me. I'm losing my ability to take things slow as she writhes beneath me on the cushions. I reach behind her to release the bra and it falls with a whisper to the rug.

Now both hands are on her, kneading the soft breasts. Her hands come around my biceps, holding on. Non-strenuous, I remind myself as I grasp the band of her underwear. I ease it down and follow the path with my mouth.

She opens wide for me, and the first taste of her is glorious and wet. The endorphins will be good for her, I reason, even as I worry about the bandage on her side.

But her body rises to my tongue and I flicker it across her sensitive bud. Her hands move to my hair, holding on, moving with me.

I keep it easy, gentle, light. I nudge her up slowly, nothing hard or fast. Still, she shifts against me, faster, with more pressure. I slip a finger inside her, knowing just where to touch her.

And she goes over, crying out, the synthetic walls absorbing her sound. I hold her tight, keeping her safely against me, feeling the pulsing against my tongue. It goes on and on, like a heartbeat against my mouth.

When she finally relaxes, I let her down softly, carefully, with ease.

Her eyes are closed. Her pale body on the bright chair is arresting. She lets go of me and moves her hand to her side.

She's had enough, I know. I lift her against me and sit on the chair, holding her tight in my lap. She turns her head into my chest. I can feel the grief flooding her now as she comes down, the crash after the high.

"No one can hear you," I tell her. "If you're upset and holding it in, you don't have to do that here."

She doesn't move, just remains tucked against me. She doesn't cry or wail. She holds on, and I keep her there, cursing the network that we both love that somehow seems set against her.

9

MIA

My instructions say to report to archives at eight. I pass through the silo entrance security a few minutes early in case I have trouble figuring out where to go.

Jax was true to his word, and I'm restored to my status as a special, cutting through back hallways and secure areas to get to the dregs of the silo, sixteen floors below the surface.

I would have taken the stairs to help with my nervous energy, but the ache in my side is pretty tremendous with nothing but ibuprofen to keep it down. I don't want to take anything stronger and have my brain fuzzy on the first day.

Plus, my blood is monitored with the implant, and I don't want my record showing I'm not tough. I don't really care what the medic said about being sensible and that pain can be more debilitating than the drug. I want all my senses about me.

I step out of the elevator with two minutes to spare. In front of me is a tech hub. It doesn't look too bad. Ten information specialists in mint-green uniforms work before oversized glass monitors. The room is bright, and the faces of the techs are focused as they move their hands along the giant clear panes full of projected data.

They sit on tall gray chairs with low backs. The seats move with them, adjusting to keep them comfortable and ergonomically safe. It seems nice. I can do this.

I walk along the tall glass screens, watching everyone. A few of them smile and nod, then refocus on their monitors. I see an empty gray chair and wonder if it is mine. Nobody's sent me a uniform. I'm still in Phase One unspecified white.

I'm supposed to check in with a woman named Ava Manning. Her image is on my watch so I can spot her. Brown hair. High cheekbones. I'd guess in her fifties. She looks like she could have modeled, with her regal angular face.

"Archivist Morrow?" calls a voice from behind me.

My heart sinks a little at my new designation. I liked Operative Morrow so much better. But this is where I have to be for now.

I turn around. "Yes?"

It's her. She holds out her hand. "I'm Archive Director Manning, but down here we don't really do the formalities. So call me Ava."

She seems kind. I relax a little bit. This won't be so bad. A big open room. Things to do. Maybe if I pay close attention to the data in my hands, I'll spot something that will give me an in. If I can prove myself—

"Are you all right?" she asks.

I've been daydreaming. "Yes," I say quickly. "Thank you."

She leads me back through the maze of screens. We're walking away from the empty chair. Maybe it's hers.

"I tried to review your records this morning, but they have all been cleared," she says. "I see you are designated as a special in the system."

"Yes. My parents were Vigilantes, but I was declared a special at their death."

She nods. "Well, this is a first for me. It's very intriguing to have someone come in without a digital past. Are you new to the silo?"

"I did my Phase One training in Tennessee," I explain. "I came to Washington for my qualifying mission. With AnneMarie Wash." As soon as that is out of my mouth, I wish I hadn't said it. Now she can check with her and get a big dose of my trainer's disdain.

"So that didn't go well?" Ava asks. Her voice is still kind.

"I failed the mission," I say. No use hiding it. "So I was sent here."

She pauses. "What was your area of specialty?"

"Infiltration, negotiation, high-pressure decision-making." I'm almost embarrassed to say it. It's like they expected the best of me, but I showed them my worst.

I look around at the smooth walls and ceiling of the corridor we are passing down. There are no doors. Strange.

"Well, I'm sorry that did not work out for you."

She gestures to the hall as we continue walking. "We call this the hall of doom," she says with a laugh. "It feels like a tunnel to nowhere."

I glance behind. We've come a long way. "What's behind all these walls with no doors?"

"Sealed archives," she says. "All the data storage for all the syndicates. It's replicated in its entirety here."

"On machines?"

She smiles faintly. "Yes and no. We don't have to actually understand the system to work with it."

We finally come to a portal. "You have access to this door as well as a break room a little farther down." She points down the hall of doom and I spot another bubble in the smooth wall. "You can also pass back through the information hub the way you came in." She steps close enough that the scanner activates, crossing its green beam down her body.

"Director Ava Manning," the door says. "Admitted."

She passes through, then the light turns red. "Please wait to be scanned," the door says.

Old tech. Slower than the ones upstairs.

I wait until it identifies me and follow Ava inside.

This room is wholly different from the hub. It's small and claustrophobic. Three low chairs sit in front of a long, wide glass screen. All are empty.

"Will I be alone in here?" I ask.

"No, we have another archivist," Ava says. She frowns. "She must be in the break room. We're still waiting for a third to be appropriated."

She moves to the far chair. "This will be your station. Give it a try."

I come around the screen and sit in the chair. It's a little low and my injury immediately protests how scrunched I feel, but I can adjust the settings later.

"Your job isn't terribly complex." Ava touches the bottom right corner of the screen and the clear pane is filled with bracketed codes of numbers and letters. "Over here"—she gestures to the right— "you have the codes for information to be removed." As her hand hovers over them, they glow various colors: blue, red, green, orange.

She points to the center. "Here, you have the actual data. A live script will run to excise these codes from the data. Your job is to make sure there are no glitches, and to compare the new and old screens to make sure the cleaned-up data is intact and sent to the correct storage facility."

"So I'm just monitoring an automatic purge?"

"You will look at the color of majority on the purge and determine a storage facility," she says.

"Couldn't that be automated?"

"We like an actual human to verify that the assignment makes sense." Ava swipes the data set upward to show raw code. "Watch it run."

The code brightens with colors as the data to be removed is matched in color. Most of it is orange, but there are a few blues.

"This is pretty cut and dried," Ava says. She pushes the data set over to an orange container like a toddler sorting blocks. "But some will require a judgment call. Like this." She passes another set of data through. This time it is half red, half green.

"The warmer the color, the more essential it tends to be. So reds and oranges trump blues and greens. A split would go to the warmer side."

"But what do the colors and codes mean?" I ask. "How can I know what facility is best?"

"That isn't essential information," she says, her voice still kind. "If you aren't sure at all, or if the color spread is just too diverse, flag it here." She presses a blinking "X" on the upper right.

I want to protest that this is something a child

could be trained to do, but it isn't the time. It's my first day. Maybe it will get more complicated later.

"If you forget the rules, tap here and they will remind you." She hits a green question mark near the bottom of the pane. "All the data you do today is just a test module. It will tell you if you did it correctly at the end of each pass. I'll check on you and make sure everything is going well." She steps away from the monitor.

I want to groan but manage to say, "Thank you."

When she's gone, I look over the screen. I'm dropping colored codes into colored boxes, and not even for real. For practice.

I run through a data set that has mostly green codes and shift it over to the green box. I'm congratulated with a check mark.

Great.

I lean over to look at the bottom of my chair. The back is too far forward, which is squishing my belly and killing my surgical site. There is a lever, but when I pull it, I drop almost to the floor.

About six places scream in agony at the sudden movement. I stand up and maneuver the chair from behind. It only goes up or down.

I jerk on the seat back, trying to get it to shift.

Are we supposed to sit on the very edge? I ram it with my elbow.

The pod door opens with a hiss. I stand up, expecting either Ava or my new coworker.

But when I see who it is, my face flames.

It's Katya, a Phase One Trainee I met the very first time I entered a silo with Jax, back in Missouri.

When I stole her shoes.

I sit on my chair. "Katya! What a surprise."

She plops down into the far chair. "Mia? Wow. Didn't figure I'd see you in archives hell."

I shrug. "You never know where you're going to end up."

"Didn't you finish your training?" she asks.

"Yes." I decide not to beat around the bush. "I failed my qualifying mission."

She flips on her screen. "So did I."

"Really?"

"Yeah. Doesn't matter. If I couldn't keep my shoes around a civilian, then I really didn't have what it takes to be a field operative."

My face heats up again. "I'm sorry, Katya. I was just trying to escape."

She swipes a set of data over to a container. Her screen looks just like mine. "It is what it is."

Katya works through a few screens. I wonder how long she's been here, and if this is all we'll ever do. I load a new set of data. Half blue, half green. Which is warmer? I send it to the blue.

A big "X" comes onscreen. "Try again," it reads.

Katya suppresses a giggle, and I have to bite my lip. I send the data to the green box.

"Don't worry," she says. "We're not doing anything important. We're redundant to the computer algorithm."

"What do you mean?" A new data set arrives, and I correctly send it to the orange box.

"My theory is that they just need to keep us somewhere so we don't go rogue. Bitter over failing our qualifier. It's a nothing job."

"Ava said there were judgment calls."

Katya snorts. "We have data for the entire global network down here. Bank transactions. Cell-phone recordings. Building permits. Birth certificates. Court cases. Money laundering. Criminal records. For a billion people. You think two archivists are really purging that data?" She snorts again. "We're banished."

"Surely there are more of us somewhere."

Katya swipes her data toward a green box. "Maybe. But there couldn't be enough of us walking through this silo shoulder to shoulder, nonstop, twenty-four hours a day to handle even a small fraction of the data."

She spins her chair to face me. "We're just pointless worker bees. Has-beens."

I move a set of mostly blue data to its box. My hand is shaking. "How do we get out of here?" I ask.

"We don't," Katya says. "I've already requested six transfers. Twice they threw me a bone and let me retest for specialty. But it always points to information archives. Rigged." She swipes her data away. "My only choice is to leave the network."

I examine the set of data in front of me. It's a mix of blue and green and orange. I hit the "X." A green check mark appears. "Good call," it adds, as if I had completed a hard one.

"You think this is dummy data, then?" I ask. "It doesn't look like cell phones or banks or crime data. It's just letters and numbers."

"It's coded. Some things do repeat. There are dates mixed in. And sometimes a cluster of things that look like Vigilante activity."

I stare at my next set. The removed data is all red. Four of the codes are the same at the beginning, but then change for the last eight digits. The smattering of other colors also end in the same digits. So these were all bits of data about the same people? Or the same thing happening to different people?

Katya looks over at me. "Trying to puzzle it out?" she asks. "Trust me, I've tried. It's pointless."

She rolls closer to me. "But one thing makes it interesting. I assign something funny to some of the codes." She swipes my data away. The next set is mostly green. "See here, these first four letters are common. YRSU. So I call it 'You really screwed up.'"

She points at all the green YRSUs with varying numeric sequences. "Lots of people screwed up this day."

This does make me laugh. We shove the data aside. The next screen is mainly orange.

"Oh, this one," Katya says. "WSRF. I call it 'Wore something really fugly.'"

"Lots of fugly on this screen," I say. I swipe it to orange.

Katya rolls back to her side. "What I don't get is

why there are only four colors. Seems like there are a lot more variations on crime or data or whatever. But if that's how we code the severity, or I guess, the lack of importance, then that's what it means."

"I don't think they'd purge big stuff, like crime or bank info," I say. "This has to be stuff like email spam or magazine subscriptions or grocery lists."

"Probably," Katya says. "I just know there are patterns."

"You think these numbers at the end are people?"

"Or businesses or institutions or types of data. Who knows?" Katya stabs at her screen. "I just know I can't do this forever."

I shove more data into a box and wonder if I can even do it a day.

10

JAX

For all the data it contains, the Vigilante database can be surprisingly bereft of useful information. Usually at the most inconvenient of times, too.

Like now.

I turn away from my screen and exhale in frustration. Ever since Mia got reassigned, I have been hunting for a new placement for her. Something that plays more to her strengths and talents, and stays clear of demolition work. The demerit in her record does her no favors in that department.

But all my searching has turned up nothing. No silo has an open position for a Phase One with her particular skill set and training. No silo except this one, of course, and AnneMarie made sure Mia was not in the running.

I tease myself by briefly entertaining the fantasy of revenge on that woman. Reassigning AnneMarie was within my authority, but the political fallout would be enormous. The network was just getting back to some sense of stability after Sutherland, the previous head of the US syndicate, attempted to take over the entire worldwide Vigilante network. The kind of power play on display by removing a high-level mission trainer for what amounted to doing her job would be terrible for morale.

The Vigilantes don't need that. And I don't need the headache that would come with justifying the move. Besides, I know Mia. She wants to do this on her own.

No, not wants. Needs. She needs that legitimacy, that sense of belonging. If I were to start pulling too many strings, she wouldn't feel as though she owned her accomplishments. She would forever be "Jax's girl."

I can't think of a worse insult to her.

I absently scroll through open positions and needs of the various silos. Nothing has changed since the last time I ran a query. I'm about to get up and hit the gym when my finger stops next to a single word: Missouri.

Of course. Director Carter.

Mia may not want me to throw around my weight on her behalf, but she never said I couldn't ask someone else to. And what better person than Carter to rescue her from the doldrums of archives?

I look at the secure communications pod, but dismiss the temptation to do this the easy way. I don't trust that thing anyway. No, better to have this meeting face to face.

* * *

Twenty minutes later I'm on a jet. The aerial view of D.C. drops away as we cruise over the suburbs and beyond, thankful as always for a chance to escape the confines of the silo.

I always did feel more comfortable out in the field than behind a desk. That week with Mia last year was one of the best experiences of my life.

Even if I did have a kill order on my head for most of it. Moving from place to place, living on our wits off the grid.

The flight at Vigilante speed takes only an hour. After a quick drive in a custom BMW not too different from my friend Colette's, I approach the rusted chain-link gate of the Missouri silo shortly before lunch. The calm female voice of the car's computer warns me that automated defensive systems have locked on to my vehicle. I cancel the BMW's stealth mode, and within seconds the computer gives me the all-clear.

I step out and wait. Within a few seconds the rusty-looking gates slide open with surprisingly little noise. I tell the car to drive itself in and park, then walk to the silo door. It opens as I approach, and a familiar blond man fills the doorway.

"Hello, Paulson," I say, and extend my hand in greeting.

"Director De Luca," Paulson replies. His voice is neutral, but I catch a glimpse of malice behind his eyes. He takes my offered hand after a pause. His grip is strong.

I bet he even thinks it's intimidating. I let the barest hint of amusement show on my face.

Paulson blinks first and lets go. "To what do we owe this unexpected visit?"

"I'm here to see Alan Carter," I reply.

"I see. And you couldn't call because…"

A flame of anger flickers inside me. "I do not have to explain myself, operative. I am here to see Director Carter. Please inform me as soon as he is available."

Paulson takes a step back as his senses seem to overpower whatever grudge he still held from last year. We crossed paths more than once. Most of those times did not end well for him.

He frowns for a second. I assume his earpiece is barking commands. "Y-yes, sir, excuse me," he says to someone on his com line. Probably Carter reading him the riot act.

Finally, he steps aside. "Director Carter is available right now," he says. "Do you require an escort or —"

I wave him off. "I remember the way. You are dismissed, operative."

I brush past him without waiting for a response. The glass panels of the entry hall light up but only display the one important piece of information about me: Head of Syndicate.

I almost liked being a fugitive better. More interesting. I stride to the end of the hall, my dress shoes clacking out a steady cadence. The door opens silently as I approach. No one asks for my weapons.

I wouldn't give them over even if they did. A perk of my position.

I pass through empty halls and enter the central silo. Terminals along the walls display a wide variety of information. Operatives move between them with the casual grace of experience. None of them pay me any mind.

This is the difference between the D.C. silo and a field silo. It makes me miss fieldwork even more.

"Jax!"

I turn toward the voice and see Alan Carter heading toward me. His smile is warm and genuine as we shake hands.

"Can I still call you Jax, or am I stuck with Director?" he says.

"That depends. Are you going to try to kill me?"

"Low blow. I didn't even try the first time."

"Point taken," I say. "Jax is fine." I look around at the other Vigilantes. None have turned toward us, but I know some are listening. "Got a place we can talk that's not an interrogation room?"

"Of course, my office is much more comfortable. Besides," he adds with a knowing laugh, "I don't really want to replace more destroyed system components."

I did leave a bit of a path of destruction last time I escaped this silo as a fugitive.

Carter walks me to his office, a small but tastefully furnished room not far from the main interior chamber. He offers me a chair, then Carter clears his throat. "I know you didn't fly all the way out here just for some southern hospitality."

I decide direct is the best route. "I need a favor, Alan."

Carter raises his eyebrows. "Now that was unexpected." He leans back in his chair. "That's it, a favor?"

"That's all."

"Well, hell, Jax, you got us all worked up for nothing. Here we thought our new syndicate head was coming for a surprise inspection." He grins at me. "Jeez Louise. Why didn't you just call?"

My watch buzzes and I take a quick glance at it. It's not important, so I brush the message away. "I prefer the personal touch."

Carter studies me in silence. "It's for Mia, isn't

it?" he asks. "I saw she failed her qualifying mission for the D.C. spot. It hasn't happened a lot to my Phase Ones."

I nod. "She won't let me pull rank, and I can't find any open positions that would be a good fit."

"Ah," he says with his own nod. "AnneMarie's reputation precedes her." He leans in, his tone mock conspiratorial. "Paulson's her contemporary, you know. They went through the program together."

"Those two are perfect for each other," I say, "but I hope you're not suggesting I swap Mia for Paulson."

"Oh, no, no need for that. I wouldn't be that mean to Paulson, anyway." He picks up a glass from his desk and rattles the ice. "But... I think I may have something coming up that would suit Mia. Fieldwork, even. I could reclassify it as a qualifier."

"Oh?"

"Nothing fancy, mind you. Just as an accompaniment to another operative."

This could work. "What's the mission?"

"There's a group of brainiacs in Nashville working on AI development. Secretive lot. We don't really suspect anything, but their intranet is totally air-gapped."

He spreads his hands apart to emphasize the point. "No outside network connections."

I understand the implications. With no Internet connection, the Vigilantes have to rely on more old-fashioned means of access. Usually this means a company plant or mole, but if that won't work, then someone has to knock a chink in their network armor.

"So you need Mia and the other operative to get in, install a network snoop, and get out."

"You got it," Carter replies. "And we only need one installed, so two people increases our chance of success on the first run-through. She can either do it herself or act as the distraction." He takes a sip of his drink and sets the glass aside. "So what do you think?"

Mia is very good at misdirection. My mind turns to all the times she managed to slip a knot around my wrist in bed without my knowing.

"I think," I say, "you've got yourself a Vigilante."

11

MIA

Day two in hell.

I wave at the happy, focused information techs who get to sit in the big open room with their huge, pretty glass panes and fancy space-age chairs.

I'm not bitter.

Or at least I can fake not being bitter.

Nobody seems to think less of me that I'm heading down the tunnel of doom to the crummy hidden archives where nobody ever visits, and I do the work a kindergartner could manage. They smile and wave like I'm one of them despite my banishment and my white Phase One outfit.

Katya is already there, sipping a latte and tossing data into boxes. She's in mint green, at least. Maybe it takes time to get the suit.

"You're on the ball and working early," I say, dropping my pack on the floor and once again examining the chair to find some way to shift the seat back.

Katya shrugs. "Early bird getting the worm. Not that I want the worm."

Something about her tone seems off, but I let it go. I'm surprised she is as nice as she is, given that I'm the one who probably got her here. Having your training shoes stolen by a civilian isn't a good mark on your Vigilante scorecard.

But having done it didn't help me any. If anything, antics like that set everyone's expectations too high.

I kick the crank on the bottom of the seat. Surely there is some way to adjust this butt trap.

Katya sighs and spins in her chair. "You know, you can just move the middle one over."

I look at the seat between us. "It doesn't belong to anybody?"

"Not until someone else draws the short straw."

She turns back to her screen.

I drag the problem chair to the middle and switch them out. When I sit in the new one, it's instantly better. "Thanks," I say.

She doesn't answer.

I spin to my screen and touch it to power it up. A message fills the entire glass. "Congratulations, you have completed your test phase successfully. Your archives will now go live into the information network."

It's silly, but I surge a little with pride. I mean, sure, a kindergartner could drop orange code into an orange box, but still, it was something I hadn't screwed up.

Katya is engrossed in her screen, so I stare at the message a moment, then finally push it away. My first round of data appears, only a few of the codes turned blue. Huh. Maybe we don't throw out as much data in real life as they showed me in the test. I send the code to the blue container.

I glance over at Katya's screen to see if hers has as little colored data as mine, but the angle isn't right to really see. I lean back a bit in my chair. Her data is almost completely black. I can't see any colors.

She's looking at it pretty intently. Then I see her touch one code, and it turns white.

"Hey!" I say. "Yours isn't computer sorted!"

She jumps a little and pushes the data offscreen. Her next set is full of green and blue, like mine. She doesn't even acknowledge that I've talked to her.

My face burns as I focus back on my own data set. I don't know anything about what I'm doing down here. Maybe later I will also get different colors and the ability to alter data. Whatever the situation is, Katya clearly doesn't want to chat.

I spend an hour mindlessly moving data. Katya gets up. "Headed to the break room," she says. The coldness in her voice alerts me not to tag along.

"Have fun," I say.

She heads out. I don't think about it for even two seconds, but dash over to her chair to peer at her monitor. She's shut it down.

She didn't do that yesterday. I distinctly remember asking her if I should power down, and her saying it didn't matter because nobody was cleared to come in the room but us and Ava.

I touch the screen, but it beeps angrily at me. "Archivist Morrow is not authorized on this security pane." A huge red "X" fills the glass.

So it knows us by touch. I hustle back to my chair. Surely it will reset. But as I do more of my information sorting, the X remains.

Crap. She'll know I touched it.

Sweat prickles on my brow. Should I call Jax? Maybe his people could clear it.

No, I can't admit this to him. I'll either have to own up to it with Katya or find another way.

I head to the entrance pod. The door slides open and I peek into the hall. It's empty, a long curving corridor of silence.

I move toward the break room. I had lunch there yesterday with Katya. She was a lot more amicable then compared to today. Maybe something happened last night. Maybe she didn't like working with me. Maybe she could slack off all day alone in there, and my presence meant she had to do more work.

The scanner blinks over the entrance pod to the break room. I pop through, planning to make a joke about my pathetic bladder, since the bathroom is inside.

But she's not there.

The room is pristine, an empty counter between the sink and refrigerated cabinet. Six egg-shaped white chairs are perfectly positioned around the long table.

I head back out. I went no farther than this yesterday, but today I decide to take a short walk and see if there are other entrances. The slight curve hides anything that might be down the hall.

I glance back a time or two as I wander along the corridor. It's eerie how perfectly the walls curve into the arched ceiling. The light beaming up from a seam at the floor is bright white on cool blue, like we're inside an ocean tunnel. The silence is complete.

I don't see any doors, but eventually I hear a murmur. I slow down, hand pressed against the wall. It's people talking. Maybe I've just come full circle and will be back in the main entrance with the tall chairs and pretty glass.

Still, I advance slowly. The curve is subtle and there is nowhere to hide.

After a few more steps, I see movement and take a step back. Now the voices are more distinct.

First an older woman, her voice quivery. "You got it all sorted?" she asks.

Then Katya. "It's harder to do with the other tech in there."

"Does she seem nosy?"

"She did look at my screen."

I slink back another step. Great. Wait until she sees the big "X" on her glass.

"I trust you can handle this, Katya," the old woman says.

"Why don't you just let the committee know you can't do it anymore?"

This gets my interest. The Vigilante committee? The big shots? I met them all a year ago, during a disaster where one of the members was killed.

"It isn't time," the woman says. "There's too much volatility in the network still." She pauses. "I'm very grateful for your work and your discretion."

No wonder Katya doesn't mind the brain-numbing work. She's doing something on the side!

I have to see who this is. I inch forward, slow step by slow step. I see their shapes again, a shadow on the floor. Just a little more.

I spot Katya. She has her back to me. But when I get closer, all I can catch is a black shoe when my shadow catches their attention.

"Is someone there?" the older voice asks.

I sprint back into our room like hell is on my

heels. The pod door is slow, and I sweat it out, sure Katya and her mystery friend will arrive.

But they don't. The door opens and I dive inside.

Still quiet.

The door closes again.

I walk around to our seats. The giant "X" still sits on Katya's computer, bright as blood smear. Great. Great.

I sit on my chair, trying to figure out what to do, my heart racing. Stupid curious me. I should know better.

I see Katya approaching the pod door and jump up, ready to confess that I touched her screen.

But then I know what to do.

"My turn!" I say. "Been holding this pee forever!"

She narrows her eyes at me.

I stand up. "I'll power yours up." I touch her screen.

I jerk my hand back when the screen beeps and says, "Archivist Morrow is not authorized on this security pane."

"Oh!" I cry out as Katya lunges for the screen. "So sorry!"

Katya touches the "X" and pushes it away. "No big deal."

I head on out the pod door. "See you in a few!"

When I get out in the hall, I take a moment to press my hand against my chest. So I got out of that one.

Is the other woman still in the hall somewhere? I move rapidly past the break room and down the corridor. Everything is silent. I walk and walk and walk until I'm most certainly past the point where she and Katya had met.

But there's nothing. No one. No doors. Just endless smooth walls.

This can't go on forever. I should ask Jax to see a map of the silo and where this leads.

Last night, I was too tired to go into what I'd been through in archives. But tonight, I would have questions.

12

JAX

My meeting with Carter ran me late on the work I had to do back in D.C. I send Mia home ahead while I fiddle with bureaucracy. One is a meeting with two trainers about a potential Phase Ten. Since Tens are rare, their performance and training are reviewed at the top level. Which now is me.

The other is a face-to-face with Olivia Beauchamp, a member of the Vigilante head committee who is still angry about the fiasco last year when her friend and fellow committee member Duran Hoffman was killed.

She inches into my office with her walking cane. The security falls away for her. She's one of only a handful of people whose clearance is actually higher than mine.

"Jax," she says by way of greeting as she sinks onto the sofa.

I leave my desk to move closer. "Hello, Olivia," I say. "To what do I owe this delightful visit?"

She waves her hand at me. "Cut the romance, pretty boy." She shifts her long pink skirt around her legs. She's eighty, easy, and her Vigilante years show in her difficulty in getting around after hundreds of missions as a weapons expert. She's been shot something close to forty times.

I have a hell of a lot of respect for her tours of duty, but she is a difficult woman to deal with these days.

"How can I help you, then?" I prop an ankle on one knee and wait. I know she'll take her sweet time getting to the point.

"I was always opposed to committees," she says, waving a crooked finger. "If you can't trust the person doing the job, then you certainly don't need a bunch of people arguing about it."

I settle in on the chair. It's going to be a long

one. I glance at the clock. Mia's been home an hour. I picture her curled up on the corner of the white leather sofa, her feet tucked beneath her.

"…But since you seem to have no interest in dissolving this stupid committee, you should at least listen."

"I have been," I say. This is our third meeting on the same topic since I took over.

"Something must be done about Operative Lukova," she says.

I want to wince at the mention of Jovana. She was the one directly responsible for Duran's death.

"We have a standing order for her apprehension," I say.

"That's not good enough!" Olivia tries to stand in her indignation, but falls back on the sofa.

I lean forward and extend my hand.

Olivia refuses my assistance and pushes herself up with her cane. She was a tall woman before she began to get stooped, and even now her eyes almost reach mine. "Jax, that woman should not have designation as a special. It keeps her hidden."

"Not anymore," I say. "We continue to monitor for her heat signature. She can't hide that. She'll turn up."

The woman stamps her cane on the polished floor. It rings through the room. "I'm opposed to the whole system," she cries. "It should go!"

I'm tired. This meeting is going to end now. "I will definitely look into it. So lovely seeing you again, Olivia."

She is undeterred. "Mark my works, Jax, if you don't remove the specials, we'll have an uprising on our hands."

I escort her to the door. "This is a point you've made very clear," I tell her. "But we're not throwing the baby out with the bathwater just yet."

That same special status that makes it difficult to track Jovana is what protects Mia. And my brother, which is even more essential now that I'm head of syndicate. My parents are longtime Vigilantes and can handle themselves, even in retirement. But Arthur turned down a position in the network and has lived as a civilian.

The young Phase Two outside my office takes over leading Olivia through the chamber. She's still muttering to herself as they head to the elevator. I turn back into my office and exit out the back, the door that will only open for me and Mia. I've had enough management work for the day. I almost wish

I could do Carter's mission with Mia. Get out in the field. Doing real work. I can't wait to tell her about it.

The drive home helps alleviate my tension. Despite the ending, the day was productive. Mia will not have to report to archives tomorrow. She'll head straight to Carter for briefing on the mission. The whole thing will take less than a week to pull off.

I turn into the complex of townhouses that serves as my home base in D.C. It's a quiet, secure set of buildings, each one set slightly apart from the others. I approach the gate and it opens to the sensor on the dash.

There are eight townhouses inside the complex, and I own them all under different names. I occupy one and keep the two on either side of mine empty of people, although outfitted to look as though they are inhabited. The other five are a base for people I trust. Four are set for Vigilantes, including Sam and Colette when they visit north. One was once reserved for my friend and comrade Klaus, although it is now reprogrammed to trap him should he ever return. The fourth I keep for guests of the syndicate.

The last one I maintain free of monitors for

family visits. My parents or my brother and his family. I haven't had a free moment to invite them since my return, although I remain in contact. I am eager for them to meet Mia. It's been a year already with her, plus my year in Ridley Prison, since I've seen them. I need to prioritize it.

The complex is quiet, although all the homes other than Klaus's have a set of randomized lighting and sound programs to make it seem as though people live there. The televisions turn off and on. Coffee grinds. Things occasionally bake. A thoroughly vetted maintenance crew keeps everything clean and organized and working properly.

It's my own miniature city.

But I know Mia sometimes finds it lonely. I expect that if she makes a friend or two within the Vigilante network in D.C., we can move them here if they like. Maybe this Katya person in archives.

I pull up to our garage and wait for the door to silently open.

Mia pops her head out the door before I have even stopped the engine. "I cooked!" she announces as I step out of the Aston Martin.

The scent of chicken and roasted carrots wafts

through the garage. "Smells amazing," I tell her.

She's changed out of her Phase One suit and into loose jeans and an MMA T-shirt my friend Colt McClure gave her last year. She looks delectable with her hair twisted up in a messy bun. I kiss her lightly. "How was archives?"

She groans. "Same data sets. Although today was 'for real.'"

She leads us back through the utility room and into the kitchen. "But I have so much to tell you about a secret meeting I saw!"

I sit on a tall chair at the end of the kitchen island. Two pots bubble on the stove and a loaf of crusty bread sits steaming on a platter. She really did cook. "Sounds intriguing," I say.

She lifts a lid and sniffs, then closes it again and turns around. "I saw Katya meeting with someone — she was on a committee. Do you think it could be THE committee?"

"Why would a Phase One archivist meet with a Vigilante committee member?"

"I don't know!" Mia cries. "But Katya was saying that since I was in the room, it was harder to do whatever she was doing for her."

"Did you notice anything Katya was doing?"

Mia comes around to lean against me. "Her screen was different from mine for a little while. She was touching data and turning it white. I don't do that."

"She's been there longer, though. She might have other duties."

"I know," she says. "But she seemed startled that I saw." She tweaks the hair over my ear. "You think we could monitor what she did somehow?"

Always scheming. That's my Mia. "Probably. Do you have a theory?"

Mia shakes her head. "Not a clue. But it's something more interesting than dropping orange code into orange boxes."

I pull her onto my lap. "Well," I say, "what would you think if I told you Alan Carter let me know about a mission he thinks you're perfect for?"

She goes still. "Did you meddle on my behalf?"

"Alan was your director during your training. He wants to see you in the network."

"So you meddled."

My arms snake around her waist. "Technically, Alan is doing the meddling."

"What's the mission?" Her voice is still uncertain.

"Infiltrating a group of kids building artificial intelligence. We just want to install some monitoring since they made their own intranet that we're not tapped into."

"Do the Vigilantes want to steal their inventions?"

"Nope. Just make sure they don't do anything that threatens other people, or that falls into the wrong hands."

Mia leans back against my chest, and for the first time since the day began, I feel my muscles relax.

"Okay," she says. "But do I have to blow anything up?"

I kiss the back of her ear. "No explosives."

She sighs. "Then I guess I'll do it. Since you went to so much trouble." She turns to jab small, well-placed punches playfully into my ribs. "I mean, since *Alan* did."

I snatch her hands and lift them high over her head. Before she can notice what I've done, I've twisted a dish towel around her wrists and cinched them tight.

"Nice capture," she says.

I pull her by her bound hands onto the glossy

black surface of the kitchen island. A second towel secures her to the iron handle on the drawer on the opposite side. Her chin is thrust high, her hips on the edge of my side of the counter.

"Operative De Luca," she chides. "What about dinner?"

I unzip her jeans.

"It can wait."

13

MIA

The new mission doesn't require any training. No explosions. No fires. Just studying a layout and the profiles of the two targets. Within two days, I'm in a car and en route to the location.

I watch the steering wheel of the silver Mercedes ease to the right as we take a curve. The car is using auto-drive, but not at Vigilante speed. While it takes me to the site of the mission, I go over the plan on the dash screen.

I'm not lead on this mission, but the distraction. Operative Carina, a Phase Three security tech, will be handling the delicate part. It's a qualifying mission for her too. She's hoping to move up to Phase Four.

I review the data. The Vigilantes have uncovered a company creating artificial intelligence that is getting too good, too fast. Their parts are handmade and off the Vigilante books, so they can actually hide their work.

Their internal network is also fashioned from the ground up, so we have no way to easily monitor their activity. The office is part bunker, with the majority of the operation underground. It isn't guarded so much as always being worked on. The team borders on obsession with the code.

Nothing they are doing is illegal, but the Vigilantes want to make sure that their success is controlled. The AI can't pose a threat to regular people, and it can't be sold to anyone with the power to use it for terrorism. They need to be watched.

Carina's job is to compromise their network by installing a bypass in the line.

My job is just to keep them away from where she's working.

The targets' images come onscreen. Two young

guys in their twenties. Both are good-looking in their way, fresh faced and clean shaven. There's a determined gleam in their eyes. They have no intention of selling out. A half-dozen investors have come in trying to fund them, but they've refused. Two of them were our operatives, just trying to get involved.

But these boys aren't interested in outsiders or their money.

Their backgrounds don't indicate anything nefarious. Just two geeky friends who want to control their work. They've barely had enough capital for the space and parts. A handful of people they've met along the way work with them for peanuts, excited by the work itself and not at a life stage where they have kids or mortgages.

Carina isn't making her presence known at all. I'm arriving early morning, when the majority of the crew hasn't arrived yet, having worked long into the night. The two main boys practically live there.

Since funding hasn't worked and they are suspicious of any strangers — we've sent plumbers, electricians, and even prostitutes — I'm the new tactic. Jax and Alan Carter are pretty sure I can think on my feet fast enough to give Carina some time to tap the network.

I'm posing as a friend of a girl who worked with them early on, then fell in love and moved away from the area. I know just enough about the operation to make this work, and I'm bringing them a problem — an AI project of my own that has failed.

I'm excited about this. It's face-to-face work. No explosives. No big things that can go wrong. But bona fide field-agent stuff.

My screen shows a hail from Mission Director Harlow. "Answer hail," I tell the dash.

Harlow's serious face fills the monitor. "Operative Morrow," she says. Her hair is pulled back in a severe knot. She's one of the most straitlaced mission directors in the South.

I sit up a little straighter.

"Your fellow operative has arrived on the scene. Give us a tap signal as soon as you have the targets diverted, and she'll get right in there."

"Absolutely," I say.

"You all set?" she asks.

I glance at the screen. "Everything is in place and ninety seconds to arrival."

"Good luck," she says, and the screen returns to

the images of the two boys.

I'm glad this mission doesn't require any sort of seduction or womanly manipulation. I don't think I could do it, knowing Jax might be monitoring my mission. Or even if he weren't. Despite my so-called tested-out ability to think on my feet and come up with creative solutions, I can't fake romantic interest.

But I can work with being a friend of a friend in need of someone to look over my work.

If they even open the door.

I glance out at the pines whizzing by. It's good to be close to home again. I loved Switzerland, and D.C. was exciting and fun.

But I'm a southern girl.

We arrive at the building. It's low and squat. Only two cars are parked in the cracked asphalt lot. A couple hundred feet away is a rundown Quickie Mart. There's a footpath cut from one parking lot to the other. No doubt these young tech wizards make a lot of late-night sojourns over there for snacks.

I open the car door. The smells of trees and dirt and open spaces are soothing. I get an idea and head over to the Quickie Mart. Inside, a bored woman with fiery red lipstick leans on the counter.

"Welcome," she says halfheartedly.

I look around. The shelves are stuffed with candy, chips, trail mix, and a few staples. A glass-doored cooler lines the back wall. I walk around a minute, wondering what those young men would pick up. I grab a couple five-hour energy shots and head to the counter.

"That it?" she asks.

"Do the people who work next door come over here often? I was thinking of picking up some snacks for our meeting and thought you might have noticed what they like."

She smirks. "Yeah, they tromp over here." She points at an endcap display of packaged pastries. "One of 'em has a real addiction to those honey buns. But mainly they get those." She waves at a machine on the counter with two bright circles of frozen slush moving inside.

I try to imagine myself carrying convenience-store honey buns and blue raspberry slushies over to meet these guys and think better of the whole plan. "I'll just get these," I say.

She rings them up. I shove them in my bag and head back over to the building.

Go time.

The front door is metal, scraped up and dented like it's been kicked a few times. I tug on the handle, but it's locked.

This is expected. I take a step toward an intercom that's seen better days and press a square black button. It buzzes.

Then I wait. A half-dozen birds fly overhead. I watch them swoop together and disappear into the trees. A couple cars rumble by on the road.

I buzz again. Breaking and entering wasn't part of my mission scope. If I fail, they'll come up with another plan with some other operative.

I will not fail.

Static comes from the speakers. "Whatup?" a voice says.

I try to say, "I'm Megan, a friend of Christy," but the voice interrupts me.

"Cage, is that you? Did you forget your key again?"

"No," I say. "My name is Megan."

The door clicks open.

Okay, that was easy.

I open it to a rush of air-conditioning. It's freezing inside. I tug my red college sweatshirt down to my wrists. The jeans and Converse are a great improvement over my last mission's outfit.

The front room is empty other than a dead ficus tree surrounded by a circle of dropped leaves and a few wires coming out of the walls. A hall leads out the back.

"Hello? Mark? Jesse?" When no one answers, I slip a thin magnetic strip over the door lock. This will leave it open. Then I take a few tentative steps toward the hall. I guess I can just head down to the bunker. I know the layout.

Of course I will. I tap my watch once to indicate I'm inside the building. The network buzzes my wrist in acknowledgment.

There are four small office rooms off the hall. All the doors are open. Three are empty. One has a desk with papers scattered all around, and a bunch of empty boxes. No people.

I head to the stairwell. The door squeaks as it opens.

It's lit inside with a tepid yellow bulb. I go down the stairs. There is no threat here for me, just a couple youngish men. The only real concern I have is failing.

The door at the bottom is heavy and sticks when I try to open it. I jerk on it a moment, then manage to get it open.

Outside is another hall. Down here will be a small kitchenette, a bathroom, and a big open space. I take a few steps. I hear a couple voices farther down.

I'm about to call out to let them know I'm here when my watch buzzes again. I glance down at it. The screen says, "Mission complete. Success. 130 seconds. Return to your car."

What?

I tap the watch three times for a confirmation. Is this a joke?

The screen flashes, "Return to your car."

I go back to the stairwell. Within seconds I am up the stairs and through the front room. I remove my magnetic strip and walk to my car.

The minute I'm inside, I bring up the dash screen and request a transmission to my director.

Harlow comes onscreen. "Congratulations, Operative Morrow, your mission was a success. The tech was able to tap into the wires and create a network bypass. Thank you for your service today."

"What?" I say. "I didn't even talk to the boys!"

"You got inside. You got our tech inside. The job is done. Come on home." Harlow nods quickly

129

and the screen goes black.

The car starts up on its own and begins the return drive to the silo. I'm still reeling.

I guess getting in the front door was all they needed? Maybe they thought the guys would be inside the front room but they weren't?

I don't feel any sort of accomplishment as the Mercedes flies down the highway. Did missions often go this way? As a nonissue?

My screen tells me I have forty minutes at this speed before I'll arrive at the silo. I tap the dash and send a request for Jax.

His happy face fills the screen. "I hear you did it in record time," he says. Then he sees my expression. "Mia? You okay?"

"I didn't do anything!" I say. "I just went in and then they told me to come out!"

"Two operatives have tried to chat with them and failed to make progress," Jax says. "You got it done!"

"But I didn't have to talk to them at all! Did they use the wires in the front room or something? I barely got down the stairs!"

"Nobody's been debriefed yet," Jax says. "We can find out when you get to the silo."

"Are you there?" I ask. Jax was in D.C. last night. I've been in Tennessee alone.

"Of course!" he says. "I wouldn't miss this. I arrived at the Tennessee silo a half hour ago."

"Will we go back to D.C.?" I ask. My head is buzzing that I'm done. That I qualified.

"We'll see where Harlow places you," Jax says. "But yes, I requested for you to be moved there."

I'm still at a loss about what to think or do. "Okay, Jax." I try to put on a smile. "I'll see you soon."

He rubs his hands together. "Can't wait to issue you your grays," he says. "I'll dress you in them myself."

My mouth quirks up at that. "Just so you can take them off again?"

"You know me," he says. "Come on back. I'll be here."

I switch off the dash screen and stare out the window. The light of the auto-drive beam follows the curve of the road. We jet around a tractor and two trucks. I glance down at the system settings. We're cloaked, so they won't even know I passed them.

I feel as pointless in the car as I did on the

mission. I didn't drive myself there. I didn't do anything there other than push a buzzer. And I'm not driving myself back.

I'd take over the car for manual drive except Jax is waiting for me, and in manual I'd have to drive at normal speed, tripling the time it would take.

So I don't. I just stare at the woods, feeling grumpy when I should be elated.

Was this mission rigged? Had they made it easy on purpose?

That just might be the first question I ask.

* * *

Fifteen minutes to the silo, according to the dash screen on the Mercedes.

I stretch my arms. I'm ready to be out of the car. Doing something productive. Maybe I did just complete my qualifying mission for the Vigilante network, but it doesn't feel like much.

I'll learn more at the debriefing.

The car engine hitches, and I grab the steering wheel as I peer at the dash. Is something wrong?

The guide light on the road is in place. I'm still cloaked.

The ride smooths out again, and my thudding heart slows. Just a glitch. I'll let silo maintenance know about it.

Then it does it again.

I grab the wheel. I don't feel comfortable driving 210 miles per hour if the car is malfunctioning. "Manual drive," I tell the car.

Nothing happens.

I press the override button on the screen, but still nothing.

"Switch to manual drive," I try again.

Nothing.

I hit the ignition button to kill the car engine, but it doesn't turn off.

Whoa.

"Civilian mode," I tell the car. Maybe I can at least get it to slow down.

"Civilian mode initiated," the dash voice says. At least that is working.

But the car doesn't decelerate. The trees whip by and we pass four cars.

"Remove all cloaking levels," I tell it.

"Cloaking levels removed," it says.

I can tell that this has worked because of the driver's shocked expression as I blow by a delivery van. He definitely saw me.

I'm not sure which I should do. Add the cloaking back or leave it off?

Vigilantes are supposed to be invisible when not in civilian mode. The car says it is, but it's driving too fast.

Jax would know what to do. But should I tell my mission director first? I tap the screen to start a message. It doesn't come on.

My fingers bang against the glass. Nothing.

Now panic starts to creep over me. The car is malfunctioning at high speeds. I can't communicate with anyone.

Stay calm. I try to assess what works and what doesn't.

"Time to destination?" I ask.

"Twelve minutes," the voice answers.

So cloaking and calculations are fine.

"Show me the Vigilante map," I say.

A projection appears low on the windshield. I see the roads and dots that let me know the location of other Vigilante operatives. There are three reasonably close.

Maybe I can just ride this out. After all, the car is on the road, heading to the correct place.

I sit back, trying to calm myself. It will be fine.

Then, the car careens off the road and into a wheat field.

14

JAX

Ten minutes until Mia reaches our silo and I can congratulate her myself.

Alan Carter and I sit in his office to wait. He's come down from the Missouri silo for this.

The Tennessee training silo isn't as decked out as the bigger Missouri one, but it's like home to me. I trained here myself when I was twelve. My own Vigilante qualifier was launched from this very room. Mangus Smith was the director then. He's long retired now.

Alan leans back in his desk chair, watching data

scroll on his monitor. "She did fine," he says. "Got in without issue. Left the opening for the tech. They got it done inside three minutes."

I sit forward on the sofa across the room. Mia didn't seem too thrilled about what happened. She wanted a bigger role.

This was certainly a step down from what she had done at the counterfeiting ring. But more in line with what she should be doing as a Phase One. Subterfuge, negotiations. I'd never been on board with the explosives element.

It wasn't Mia's style.

Carter's desk screen switches to video. It's Harlow, the mission director for Mia. Her face is stern and serious. "We have an outage on a network car," she says.

Carter shoots forward in his chair. "Whose?"

"Operative Morrow," Harlow says. "No communication ability. Engine volatility. She's gone in and out of cloak."

I leap from the sofa. "Who's nearby?" I ask. I want to jump in my own car, but surely someone is closer than I am.

"I have three operatives approaching her," Harlow says. "But she's at top speed. There aren't many who have the qualifications to intercept her."

"Where's Colette?" I ask. My friend in the network is a Phase Six driver and based out of the area.

Carter taps on his screen. "One hundred miles out," he says. "Not close enough."

"It is for Colette," I say, and head for the door. "Get me a vehicle ready before I'm up top," I tell him.

Carter nods.

I head down the hall, tapping my watch to hail Mia on hers. I have a direct com between us that doesn't require Vigilante network access.

She picks up. On the tiny screen, I can only see the roof of her car and part of her hair.

"Jax!" she cries. "The car is plowing through a field!"

"Can you jump out?" I ask. At the sound of her panicked voice, I take off at a run, heading for the elevator to get to the surface.

"I'm over 200 miles per hour," she says. "I didn't train for this yet. I don't know how to eject or to land."

"You want me to talk you through it?"

I hear a crunching sound and Mia screams. My

heart hits the floor. "Are you all right?" I shout, ignoring the stares of people who turn to look at me. I approach the elevator bank and press my hand to the scanner to speed up the identification. A screen lights up and I tap in the code to commandeer it.

"Mia!" I shout.

The elevator opens and I rush in. Several confused Vigilantes stand inside, looking out the open door as if trying to figure out why they are on that floor.

The elevator shoots straight up top. The others brace themselves and a couple cry out, unfamiliar with this little-known feature available only to a head of syndicate.

"I'm okay," Mia finally says. "The car is evading trees — mostly. We hit some."

The doors open and I'm out, walking through the entrance past the blinking glass screens that announce my position.

"Is it still functional?" I ask. Her face comes in and out of the screen. She's bumping along.

"Oh, yes, we are still at top speed."

"Where are you exactly?"

"I just left the highway about ten minutes out. It's a hayfield, harvested. We haven't hit any bales."

I exit the silo just as a black Maserati pulls up. The door opens. It's unmanned. I sit inside and link my watch to the dash. It reads the location of Mia's transmission and shoots forward. "I'm heading your way."

My dash screen lights up. It's Alan Carter. "Two Vigilantes are about to intercept," he says.

"Where's Colette?" I ask.

"Still five minutes out."

"Colette's coming?" Mia asks. Her voice bounces, like she is being shaken as she talks.

"You've got two Vigilantes close, and Colette is not far behind," I say to her. "We'll get you out of this."

"Does this happen to cars?" Mia asks.

"Never," I say. "It should never happen."

"I can't keep talking, Jax. I have to pay attention."

"Keep the line open," I tell her, but she's gone.

I'm torn between getting her back so I know what is happening, and doing as she asks, letting her concentrate.

My dash screen splits and Colette appears beside Alan. "Jax, I'm close," Colette says. "There can be no explanation for her car other than code."

"You think someone fed the car bad directives?" I ask.

"Had to." Her French lilt is gone today, all serious. "I'll get her."

"I'm fifteen out," I say. "She's heading away from me now."

"Don't worry, Jax," Colette says. "I won't let anything happen to her. I'll report back." Her screen blips out.

I want to smash my hand on the steering wheel that I can't get there. I should have stayed close, like I did on her last mission. There is no way this was an accident. First the explosion. Now her car.

Carter's screen is still active. He's watching me. "I know where you're going with this," he says. "We're going to investigate. We'll get her. We'll put her somewhere safe. And we'll get to the bottom of it."

I watch the world whip by. "That's not good enough," I growl. "There is no reason for anyone to go after Mia."

Carter rubs his forehead with the heel of his hand. "Actually, Jax, there must be. This is two questionable inside problems within a week. We'll have to figure it out."

I want to drive myself, slam the accelerator, but I know we'll get there faster if I let the car do its job.

Mia has to be okay. She has to.

15

MIA

The minute I let Jax off the communication line, I regret it.

The car is totally freaking out, weaving across the edge of a field, occasionally drifting into the tree line then back out again.

I grab the wheel, but it's useless. It turns on its own, its movements too forceful for me to stop with my bare hands.

I periodically tap on things, trying to get something to come back on line. I can't kill it. I can't brake. I can only do superficial commands like cloaking or maps.

It also still dispenses drinks from the center console. So I won't be thirsty if I die.

Not that I could swallow anything from the Mr. Pibb that popped up when I asked for it, just checking functionality. We're bumping along the rutted field. We get too close to a giant roll of hay and scrape the side. It tumbles over.

The car heads toward the trees again and I suppress a scream as we mow down a fence. We swerve right to left and I don't know if the car is purposefully dodging the big ones or if I'm getting by on dumb luck.

We come out on the other side of the forest to a road, and I see a police car with its sirens and lights going. I panic. He can't help me, and he really doesn't need to be seeing this car. Probably somebody reported me while I wasn't cloaked.

"Initiate all cloaking!" I tell the car.

The dash doesn't answer like it usually does but we must be hard to see, as the police car slams to a stop as we blow by. In the split second as we pass, I see the officer swiveling his head, trying to see where we went.

Two cars head straight for me at high speeds.

Must be Vigilante, as they appear only briefly then become just glinting light and a blur of color. I check my dash and yes, two red blips show on my map. The blue dot of the civilian police is quickly left far behind.

"Remove all cloaking," I say. They'll need to be able to see me.

The two Vigilante cars remove theirs as well. They slow down as I approach and turn around to go the same direction. I have no idea what they are going to try. I picture attempting to jump from my car to theirs like some adrenaline-fueled action movie and yelp out loud.

I pass them, then they accelerate to catch up.

The three of us zoom down the highway now, all together. But these aren't high-level drivers, and they struggle to keep up and stay on the road. They can't use their auto-drive so close to me unless we go in single file. They drop back behind and I see their beams working the edge of the road.

I realize my car is aiming for something. We've been going roughly the same direction even with the foray into the field. It's just that the road went another way, and the car kept going the same route, like a bird would fly.

What's ahead?

I tap my watch to bring back Jax. "We're headed somewhere specific," I tell him. "I'm trying to project the location based on the direction."

"Alan's way ahead of you," Jax says. "It's a dam."

"A what?"

"The dam over Cumberland River."

"What do I do?" I ask.

I glance behind me, but the other two Vigilantes have pulled back. "Where are they going?" I ask.

"Look to your right."

I do, and I want to weep at the sight of Colette's BMW. She pulls up right beside me. Her passenger window rolls down.

My fingers fumble for the lever. Please go down, I beg the window. I know it's unbreakable, bullet-proof, and full of tech.

The Vigilante glass rolls down.

"Hello, Mia!" she shouts with a wave. "Nice day for a drive!"

"I'm so glad to see you!" I yell.

"I'm going to toss you my watch," she says. "Then you toss me yours!"

"Why?" I shout.

146

"Just do it!" she says.

Colette is good, keeping her car aligned with mine. But we are going crazy fast and my car doesn't stick to the road, beelining it for the dam with every curve and bumping into the ditch or across the fields.

"Here we go!" Colette says. She squints her eyes and throws the watch through my window.

I don't catch it, but it lands on the passenger seat and I snatch it up.

"Quickly!" she says. "Before your car blocks my identity out!"

I jerk the watch off and take a deep breath. Our cars almost bump, but Colette keeps them steady. I toss it through her window.

Her BMW veers away. My car says, "Operative Rigal identified. Initiating Phase Six driving protocol."

The engine drops off immediately, and I'm in manual mode. I grab the wheel and steer the car back onto the road. Gradually we slow down until I can safely hit the brakes.

Then I'm stopped.

I lunge out of the car and back away like it's on fire.

The other two Vigilantes pull up behind me.

One jumps out of her car, a tall blonde in jeans. "You okay?" she asks.

"Yeah," I say. "I think."

The other Vigilante gets out, a stocky man with a goatee. He peers into the car. "How'd you get it to stop?"

"We fooled it with another Vigilante's ID," I say. "She's a Phase Six, so it changed modes."

"So it was a programming problem, not a mechanical one," the woman says.

"I have no idea," I say. I'm shaking. "It started glitching, then stopped responding to my commands."

The woman puts an arm around me. "We'll get you back to the silo."

"What about Colette?" I look at my wrist to ask Jax, but realize my watch is in her BMW.

"Sounds like she can handle it," the woman says.

Another car pulls up and screeches to a halt behind the rest of us. It's a black Maserati. Both the Vigilantes' watches chime.

"Head of syndicate approaching," the man says. "What's he doing down here?"

The woman turns to look.

I don't have to. I know why Jax is here.

Me.

16

JAX

I'm out of the car in seconds. Mia is standing with two other operatives.

I don't care what they think, but pull Mia into my arms.

"Are you all right?" I ask.

She holds tight for just a moment, then pushes away. "I'm fine. Who is watching for Colette?"

"Alan's monitoring," I say.

"You think her car will be okay?"

"She'll narrow down whether it was your car or your identity causing the issue," Jax says.

This makes the blond woman whip around. "You saying she was targeted?" she asks.

"You'll be briefed as necessary," Jax says. "Thank you both for coming to her aid."

"I have to get back on my mission," the man says. He extends a hand to me. "Pleasure to meet you."

I shake his hand. Mia and I wait by the Maserati as the two of them take off again.

Then we're alone on the highway with her car and mine.

"Is Colette going to be okay?" Mia asks.

"Let's go see," I tell her. We head toward the Maserati, but Mia abruptly turns and hurries back to her car. I wait for her, still anxious about the vehicle, as she sticks her head inside. She comes back with a watch.

"It's Colette's," she says. "She had us switch."

"Alan wanted to narrow down the glitch." I take the watch from her.

"So now Colette's car thinks I'm driving?" Mia asks.

"That's the idea." We settle in the seats of the Maserati, and I flip on the dash screen.

Alan is there. When he sees me, he says,

"Colette's car also went rogue when it identified Mia. She was definitely targeted."

My jaw clenches. "Then it's an inside job," I say.

Mia gasps. "Somebody doesn't want me in the network?"

Alan frowns. "Apparently so. For your own safety, we have to keep you off grid."

"Can I come to the silo?" she asks.

"That should be safe enough for now," Alan says. "But we do need to get to the bottom of this."

"We'll head back," I tell Alan. "Get her Vigilante status revoked and have her returned to full special with zero tracking."

"Will do," Alan says. "Don't worry, Mia. We'll figure it out."

"But I don't want my Vigilante status revoked!" Mia cries. "I just earned it!" She sits back against the seat. "Actually, I don't feel like I earned it."

"You did," I say. "Even if this mission was nothing, you earned it at that vault."

"Get yourselves back here," Alan says. "We'll take a look at every parameter on both jobs. See who logged into any information database on either mission. We'll see who had clearance to know anything and could have manipulated the explosive device and the car."

"Where is Colette?" Mia asks.

Alan hesitates. "She is in the river. As is her car."

"She lost her car!" Mia cries. "Is she okay?"

"Colette is fine," Alan says. "She ejected. But whatever was attached to your identification, Mia, was powerful stuff. Phase Ten programming."

Mia looks away from the screen, staring out the window.

"See you in fifteen," I tell Alan, and power off the monitor. I initiate a specialized cloak that even locks out the network, at least the network as we know it. Who knows who has infiltrated what?

"Talk to me," I tell Mia.

She doesn't speak for a moment. She looks at the car ahead of us, silent and still, just another black Mercedes like hundreds of other Vigilante vehicles. I know how she feels. Like it betrayed her.

And it did. The whole network has.

"I'm nobody," she finally says. "An orphan who grew up knowing nothing about Vigilantes. Who didn't stand out in school and never finished junior college." She turns to me, her eyes pained. She looks young and innocent, like the college student she's dressed as for the mission. "Why would anyone want to kill me?"

I lean over the console and pull her close to me. "I'm not going to let anything happen to you," I say.

"You're not in control of it," she says. "This is inside. Like Jovana. Like Sutherland."

She's bringing up all the failures of the network from the past year. To her, the network is flawed, dangerous, caving in on itself. I want to tell her that for almost one hundred years, it's been the most stable thing in the world, the most useful, and the best.

But it's definitely got its problems now. And Mia is caught right in the middle of it all.

17

MIA

When I was a young girl, my dad used to do what he called "puttering." He'd wander the house, picking up random objects and setting them down again. Occasionally he'd look out the window at the day, which was most likely rainy or cold or else he'd be out in it.

He hated being inside. Hated normal days. He wanted to be doing something impulsive or dangerous, maybe even reckless.

I feel his presence today as I am puttering myself. Jax's townhouse is spacious and beautifully decorated. I let my hand flutter through the delicate sheer curtains that hang over the enormous floor-to-ceiling windows. I cross the room and trail a light touch over the almond suede sofa. My fingers tinkle through the glittery drops of crystals that delicately edge the shade of a gorgeous floor lamp.

What do I do now?

Jax insists I stay away from the silo and remain off grid while he and Alan Carter try to figure out who tampered with my car. And the explosive.

I press my hand to my side. The bandage is gone and yesterday Jax ordered the medics to remove the medical implant that monitored me. Another safety precaution. But I'm better. I don't need it.

It's been two days since the car incident in Tennessee, and I'm already over it. Wasn't danger the name of the game as a Vigilante? My life had been a nonstop deadly thrill ride when I first met Jax, and we'd survived every single thing that had been thrown at us.

But Jax insists this is different. An inside job that can actually get me.

So I am here.

Maybe I belong here.

I cross the living room and settle on a lovely

window seat full of soft pillows. I pull my knees up to my chin and look out on the other townhouses inside our complex. I can't see the empty ones on either side of us, but across the street is the one Jax reserves for Sam. He's due to come in later today to help figure out the tech behind the problems I had during my qualifying missions.

I'm looking forward to seeing him, however much I'm allowed.

I'm a bird in a cage.

A beautiful cage.

The window is vast, bumping out in an octagon of glass. I press my hands to it. Only a slight chill. The weather outside is mild for late fall. I'm wearing jeans and a silky gold shirt, a gift from Armond, who handles Jax's wardrobe.

I can buy anything, have any object in the world delivered to me. And sometimes I think I'll just go nuts and get everything I've ever wanted. Jewelry. Computers. Books. Clothes. A car. A boat. A plane!

But I don't do it. What I really want is to be useful. To help the network. To take whatever puny skills I possess and do something with them.

I'm not afraid that someone is trying to kill me.

No more than my father was afraid to die.

I picture my parents on their final boat ride, heading out into the storm. My mom's hair would be wild, blowing everywhere, escaping whatever tie she'd attempted to use to tame the silky blond strands. Dad would be in white, always, a sharp figure doing something critical with the sail or tying one of his intricate knots to batten something down.

For the first time in a long time, I ache for my parents. I am twenty-one now. I haven't seen them for thirteen years. But I recognize how much like them I have become.

I bang my hand against the window. It doesn't make a sound. I hit it harder. It's not regular glass, I realize, but the stuff they use in Vigilante cars. Bulletproof. Tough as steel. I smack it as hard as I can, and this time a faint beep sounds.

My watch buzzes. It's the special one, not tied to the network. Just for Jax. His image comes on the small screen. "You okay?" he asks.

It must have been the glass. He's monitoring me awfully close.

"I'm fine," I say. "I think I'm going to get out. Getting a little stir crazy."

He nods. "Why don't you check on the other houses? You'll laugh at the one on the right. It was decorated sort of as a joke, all pink and red."

I wonder whose joke it was. Jax doesn't joke. I don't know how long he has owned this set of buildings. "I was thinking of shopping or something."

"There's a computer in my office that is secure," he says. "Order anything from anywhere. It'll be delivered to an offsite facility and someone will drive it all over."

"I meant at a store. Surely there's a mall somewhere."

He nods again. "Of course. I'll send a security team over to go with you."

I look back out the window. "That's okay. I'll stay here."

"Mia?" His voice is gentle. "You're free to do anything you like. I just need you safe."

I nod but don't look at his face on the watch screen. "I know, Jax. Just let me know if any news comes along."

"Of course I will," he says. "Everybody I trust is working on it."

"See you tonight," I say, and flip off the watch.

I turn away from the window and lower my feet to the floor. I have no doubt that if I step outside, I'll be followed. Maybe I will walk around the complex. I haven't had time to really explore, between my explosives training, and the missions, and then the reassignment. Jax said I was free to do anything. I'm not locked in.

I walk through the kitchen, pick up an apple from the bowl, and take a bite as I head out through the garage. Surely this overprotection won't last forever.

I won't let it.

18

JAX

Mia can't go on this way.

I spin in my chair to face the glass screen of my monitor. Perhaps I should resign. Get us out of here. Maybe now she'll be amenable to Switzerland again.

I tap my screen to bring up the list of my things in secure long-term storage. Somewhere in this silo's guts is the ball holding the engagement ring.

But I stop.

No. I have to stay here. Figure out who is after her, and why.

My complex is safe. I don't doubt that. It was
built from the ground up for my use, and I have
three retired Vigilantes working the grounds. One is
a landscaper, but used to be a weapons specialist.
Another bakes now, and is working out of Sam's
house. She used to be a combat trainer. A third is a
security specialist going through every part of the
network connection for chinks.

All are keeping tabs on her from a distance. I've
asked them not to update me or invade her privacy.
But to watch.

I know she needs more room to roam. I'll get
her more, as soon as we figure this out.

I call up Sam on the monitor.

His face fills the screen, his grin wide. He's
buzzed his black hair. "Lookee there. It's Jax, our
head honcho. I'm about an hour out on D.C."

"What the hell did you do to your head?" I ask.

He rubs his scalp. "Looking sharp for the
ladies."

"You heading here to the silo or to the
townhouse?" I ask.

"I'm wherever you tell me to be. But I probably
like your girl better than you."

I smile. "Story of my life. You make any

headway on that data?"

"Sure, but it would take someone in code to make sense of it. Mia's car was clean. Colette's car was clean. But we knew that. Whatever they did was tied to Mia's ID."

"What about the explosive?"

"Well, that evidence went up in smoke, but the data still looks clean. Could have been something that reversed itself before the boom, though. Without the device, we don't really know."

"Has anybody found Jovana?"

"Off grid, boss. Just as invisible as she always has been. You think it's her? She would have to have someone inside."

"I don't doubt she does," I say. "But it's not her style."

"Agreed on that one. She's a lot more hands-on."

The corner of my screen pulses with a message from the assistant who works the front desk of my office. Someone is waiting for me outside. "Keep at it," I tell Sam. "See you tonight."

He salutes and signs off.

I click the message from the Phase Two who controls who gets in to see me. Apparently Olivia

Beauchamp is here, requesting another meeting. Another round about the evil of specials and my failure to apprehend Jovana, no doubt.

I tap out, "Send her off," and head for my back entrance. I'm not up for wasting time on Olivia today.

The secure hall is silent and empty. I feel about as isolated as Mia must, even though I'm surrounded with people. The network is in real trouble, and it's happening on my shift. I need a plan. A team. A trustworthy group.

Sam will be here. I could get Colette.

For the first time in a while, I think of my parents. Dad was a top-notch mission strategist in his day. Mom was a Phase Four seductress until he came along, which I didn't like to think about. When she decided to have my brother, she moved over to interrogation.

These are handy skills, even if they are retired.

I circle back through security, killing time. Calling them is an excellent idea. We're due for a visit. They can meet Mia. We can strategize, the four of us. Maybe I can even get my brother, Arthur, to come up with his wife and two boys.

This would help in every way.

By the time I make it back to my office, Olivia is long gone. I send off secure messages to my parents and to Arthur, and start scrolling through the day's tasks.

The notification icon on the bottom of my monitor goes off again.

Great. She's back.

I click on it.

But it's not Olivia's data that loads onscreen.

It's Katya, the Phase One Mia worked with in archives. The one she stole the shoes from when we escaped from the Missouri silo.

What's she doing here?

I bring down the entrance security.

"Come in," I command.

She steps in tentatively. She looks scared to death in the mint-green archives uniform. I wonder what specialty she attempted in her Vigilante qualifier. She's definitely ballsy if she managed to convince someone to give her an appointment with me.

"Archivist Reynolds," I say, standing from behind my desk. "What brings you to my office?"

"Is Mia okay?" she asks. She stands near the door as if she's afraid to come any closer.

My senses go on alert. "Is there reason to believe she isn't?" No one with less than level-six clearance knows of the incidents with Mia inside the network. We've contained the data.

"She quit coming to the archives," she says. Her voice has a quaver in it.

I relax at this. "Mia was transferred to a more suitable position," I say. "Thank you for your concern. I'll have her message you if it will make you feel better."

I turn back to my screen to signal that our conversation is over. But the girl doesn't move.

"Is there something else?" I ask her.

"It's just..." She walks forward like my desk is an execution chamber and drops a tiny microchip on the shiny surface. "I thought you should see this."

I scoot it closer to me. Nobody uses physical memory in the upper levels of the silo. Must be an archives tool. "What is its significance?"

The girl bites her lip. I wonder who the hell did her Phase One training in subterfuge. No wonder she's in archives. She has the poker face of a kitten.

"I have been doing some...extra work," she says. "In the archives. It was all coded so I didn't know what it was. But on the day Mia disappeared, there was, well, a flurry of code stuff to delete. Like a lot more than usual."

No telling what data she was getting fed or how old it was. But she is pretty intent on telling me about it, so I listen. "Go on," I say.

"I aligned some of the codes with other ones," she says. "And it sort of led me to believe Mia was in danger. I think something happened to her a couple days ago and the data was purged."

I lean back in my chair. This girl is smart. That is clear. Frightened and poorly trained, but she could put information together even when it was meant to be hidden.

"So you wanted to let me know?"

"I just wanted to make sure she was okay."

I pick up the chip. I don't have a way to get the data in this office. I'll have to turn it over to Sam. "So what did you see that made you think she was in danger?"

"I know Mia is a special." She shrinks a little when I whirl around at that. She quickly adds, "It was on her guest screen in the Missouri silo."

I nod. I remember that now. They identify everyone there.

"And when all that data came through," she goes

on, "I thought that maybe it was tied to specials. So I matched up codes." Her eyes go back to the chip on the desk. "And I found other similar ones. People who aren't supposed to be tracked, getting tracked, and then their tracks end."

"What was your conclusion?"

She takes a deep breath, like she doesn't want to say what she's going to say. But she does.

"Someone is killing specials."

19

MIA

I'm not stupid. I know that landscaper isn't a regular gardener. He's too fit. Too alert.

I wave to him as he prunes an already perfectly shaped bush. I'm not mad at Jax for having people watch me. He's got people here all the time, whether I'm around or not.

But I want to be my own bodyguard. I'm a Vigilante, right?

I want to be back in training. Learning more skills.

But now I can't even go to a silo.

Maybe I can at least do something with civilian trainers. There has to be something that will keep me in shape, teach me something new.

Krav Maga would work. Or I could do Mixed Martial Arts, like the fighters do.

I could search online, but I'd rather just find a place myself. There's several strip malls a few blocks down. Those types of places often have little hole-in-the-wall fitness centers or dojos. I'll see what's close, check it out. Surprise Jax that I'm going to pick up some skills while we wait on the network to figure out its own undoing.

I duck back inside the house to snatch up the civilian-looking security pass and a small bag with my alternate identification and credit cards. I glance at the image on the ID. It's not me but someone who looks like me, good enough for regular law enforcement or normal people. The credit makes a circular path back to Jax through multiple accounts. My name on this card is Carla.

I wave to the landscaper again as I wander around. To his credit, he doesn't immediately move to stop me, follow me, or even speak into a communication device to tattle on me. He just returns the greeting.

When I'm past him, I quickly backtrack and shoot through a wall of shrubs to the hidden pedestrian gate.

It looks pretty ordinary, but it's not. On the inside, it will scan my heat signature just like in the silos. But that tech is too obvious on the outside and might attract attention. So we use a clicker like any old-school garage might have to get back inside, even if the gadget uses technology that the rest of the world won't have for twenty years.

The ornate iron gate opens, and I step outside with a happy sigh. The weather is perfect, cool and breezy but not cold. Sunshine pours down as I walk along the stucco wall that surrounds the townhouses. It looks normal too, but is actually reinforced concrete and steel that can withstand a wrecking ball. Jax has made this complex his fortress.

I glance back. If anyone is following me, it's not obvious. The landscaper doesn't come out of the gate.

Maybe I'm actually free.

It takes a couple blocks to get to an intersection with any traffic. I head to the right, where I've spotted some stores before. Maybe I'll pick up something small that is all my own. After my house was destroyed back in Tennessee, I have resisted collecting things that could be lost.

But today I feel the urge to own something.

I pause at the corner and look back again to see if anyone is following me. There's a teen girl. An old lady walking a poodle. But Vigilantes are good. They are trained to go unseen. I move on toward the businesses. If they are following, it's fine. I can still roam.

The first building has a liquor store, a rug shop, and a bakery. I keep going. On the next block, there's a clothing boutique, a children's toy shop, and —

I pause. A bridal store.

Without really meaning to, I leave the sidewalk and cross the small parking lot to the storefront. I pause before the great glass window and admire the three gowns displayed there. One is beaded from collar to hips and flares out below in a burst of glittery netting. The second is long-sleeved and gleaming with smooth satin in a sheath that flows down into a long train.

The third is short and simple, a lace overlay on top of a creamy silk base.

None of them fits my style, but it's nice to pause and admire them. I tug my phone out and snap a picture of the store so I'll remember if I need it later.

When I need it, I correct myself.

Jax has been patient. He hasn't pressed me with his proposal since we left the Swiss Alps. I lean against a pole. Has he changed his mind? When he asked me to marry him, I was still the adventurous girl who'd insisted he take me along on his quest for revenge.

Now I was the wannabe operative who'd managed to become a target. I'm holed up at home.

Like a housewife.

Maybe that's what I should be. It is a good life. Many of my favorite people back in Tennessee are perfectly happy being married and raising children and keeping a home.

A woman comes up behind me. She also stops to look at the dresses, tucking a bit of her sleek black hair behind her ear. "I'm not a fan of any of these," she says, gesturing to the window. "That one would make my hips look wider than the Capitol Building." She pats her thigh.

I can't imagine her hips looking wide, as she's very slender in a gray pantsuit. But I don't respond.

"The shop has a good reputation. Are you getting married?" she asks.

I shift my naked hand self-consciously behind my back. "Maybe soon."

"You should come in," she says. "No harm in looking."

She opens the door and waits for me to go in ahead.

I hesitate, then pass by. The shop is small, both sides lined with white dresses in plastic bags. Near the back is a long counter. Empty.

The other woman heads to one of the racks. I glance at the display in the middle, which is a tree of veils, their white netting draping like a fabric chandelier.

I head to the side opposite the other woman. I'll glance through the dresses, then go.

The shop smells of fabric and roses. There are vases of flowers throughout the store, all with a stack of cards next to them. Wedding florists probably provide them as advertisement.

Planning a wedding. It hits me that I'll have to do that at some point.

Once I say yes, of course. Assuming the question is still valid.

I've made a mess of everything.

A heavyset woman pushes through a set of swinging doors in the back corner. She has a yellow measuring tape draped around her neck. "Why, hello!" she says. "Can I help you?"

Crap. Now I'm involved.

"I'm just browsing," I say. I hope she'll move on to the other lady, but when I turn to point her out, the woman isn't in the room. Did she leave? Or go back to try something on?

Strange. I'm alert now.

Then annoyed at myself. It's a bridal shop. Nobody could have guessed I'd go here.

Jax sure wouldn't have.

I walk along the dresses, arranged from short to long. It's interesting to think that I could afford any gown in this shop. Money isn't an issue. It's a weird feeling. Maybe I should just announce, "Give me one of each!"

This idea makes me smile.

"Like that one?" the shop owner asks.

Wow, she's paying attention.

I'm not even sure which one she means, but before I can comment, she whisks a dress off the rack and carries it to the back. "I'll start a room for you," she says. "What's your name?"

I hesitate. "Carla," I say. My neck prickles. Something still feels off.

"Wonderful, Carla," she says. "If you see anything else, let me know!" She disappears into the back.

I wonder if I should sneak away while she's out of sight. She seems to be the only one here midmorning on a weekday.

I'm planning to head straight out the door.

But then, I see it.

The dress is pure white, cut straight across the collarbone with a scalloped trim. It's fitted up top and then flares out. The beadwork is thick at the top and then scattered as it goes down, like stars falling.

I love it.

A lot.

I pick it up. I can try on this one dress. Leave the fake name if I like it. It will be here, ready for me.

If I need it.

When I need it.

The woman comes out while I'm walking back. "Find another?" she asks.

"This one," I say tentatively.

She takes it from me. "This sample size will be a

little big for a tiny thing like you, but slip it on and I'll come back and pin it so we can get the effect. We'll measure you for size when we order yours."

I nod. We go through the swinging doors. In the back are two curtained dressing areas on either side of an enormous set of angled mirrors.

A small sofa and scattered chairs attest to the fact that many brides bring family or friends on this type of excursion. My throat catches a little that my mother isn't here, nor my Aunt Bea. I have no one. The closest things to friends are Colette, whom I've really only met a handful of times, and Katya from archives. Though she probably hates me for escaping.

Maybe I should focus on making friends here. I just don't know where to start.

The woman pulls a curtain back to show the previous dress. She hangs the new one on a hook inside and unzips the bag. "Would you like some assistance getting into the gown?" she asks. "It can be a lot of fabric to manage."

"I'm okay," I say. "I'll let you know if I run into trouble."

"I'll be right here!" she says. "There's a buzzer on the wall if I've wandered out front."

"Thank you," I tell her.

She pulls the curtain closed.

I turn to the dress. It really is lovely. I run my hands along the fabric, cool and smooth until you reach the bumpy texture of the beads.

My watch buzzes. It's a video hail from Jax, but I don't want him to see where I am. If I turn on the screen, he'll see the dress. I'm not ready to tell him.

I deny the message request. I'll talk to him later.

I reach to take the dress off the hanger, then stop.

My neck prickles again. All senses go on alert.

I turn just as I take a blow to the temple. My head jerks to the side.

I react according to my training and spin away from the impact to reduce its force. My elbow sinks into someone as I add energy to the turn to counterattack.

A flash of black hair tells me it's the woman who convinced me to come inside. I walked right into this. Foolish. So foolish.

I clench my fist and follow the elbow with a hard strike to her chin, hoping for a concussion-level blow.

But this woman is trained too and blocks the

punch.

We're facing each other now. I want to ask her who she is, but it's pointless. She's here to finish the job that wasn't completed at the vault or in the car.

She moves to sweep my legs but I see it coming and leap into her. In my training, because I am outweighed by most opponents, I learned that my elbows are my greatest asset. I use one again to drive a hard blow straight to her neck.

The woman is off balance from her failed sweep and takes the hit. As she spins into her recovery, I realize she's not Vigilante. She isn't responding the way we are taught. And if she wanted me dead, I would be. She would have gotten me with a dart gun straightaway.

She's a civilian.

Armed with this knowledge, I use one of the standard Vigilante disarming moves, an artery pinch at the base of the neck.

The woman is surprised by this and drops to her knees. She's tough, but not trained to get out of this hold.

"Who are you?" I ask.

She's blacking out, so I ease off. I want information from her. I'm only a Phase One, but she can't measure up to me. The other attempts on my life were from inside the network.

But this one isn't. And she's terrified of who I am. No one told her I would fight back.

She unexpectedly screams, and I drop her with an elbow to the back of her head. Now it's my time to get out of here. The last thing I need is civilian police.

I lurch out of the curtained area. The shopkeeper is coming through the swinging doors. I spot a back exit and dash for it.

"What's happening?" the owner cries.

I'm already out the door. My feet crunch the broken bits of asphalt in the delivery-truck lane behind the strip of stores. I run in a dead sprint, glad to be in shape from training, feeling the adrenaline rush blast away any pain from my injuries.

So stupid. SO stupid.

My breath is precise, inhaling every few steps to keep me fueled. Should I return to the complex? Am I leading someone there? Surely they already know that's where I am. They had to have followed me.

But I don't want to take them to my door. Not just yet. I spot shoulder-high hedges ahead and now I'm superwoman, running, jumping on a fire hydrant and pushing off to leap over the squared-off bushes.

I realize as I sail over it that there is a fence hidden on the other side of the greenery. I land in the grass just inches from a concrete fountain.

It's the courtyard of some posh cafe. There are round tables with the chairs tilted against them, not yet set up for customers. I dash through them. At the other corner, I pause to see if I've been followed.

No one is visible.

The gate in the front corner is locked, but it's an easy climb up a metal trellis. Then I'm airborne again, over the fence and into a parking lot on the side of the building.

A couple cars are parked there, probably early staff to set up. I move near the wall and wait. No one is anywhere.

I don't think the black-haired woman will come around in time to follow. She seemed pretty freaked out by my skill. Nothing about that encounter says Vigilante, although maybe they hired someone they shouldn't have trusted.

I tap my watch.

"Jax!" I hiss.

When he answers, I see that he's in his car. And

he looks upset.

"You're flushed," he says. "Are you all right?"

"I just got attacked by a woman in a bridal shop."

"You were in a bridal shop?" he asks.

"That is not the important part!" I say.

"I'm coming your way," he says. "I tried to message you earlier. Someone is trying to kill you."

"Already figured that out! I got away. I'm not sure where I am." I look up for a sign. There's nothing I can see from here. "I didn't want to head home in case I was followed."

"I'm tracking you," he says. "I'll be there in fifteen."

"Too long," I say. "I'll head back if I think it's safe."

"Mia," Jax says. His tone is hard. "Let me come get you."

"I'm fine," I insist. "I'm tired of being rescued. I just wanted you to know what happened in case…in case something else happens."

"I'm close," he says. His face is dark with anger.

"I'll be fine," I say. I click off the watch. I feel elated. I was attacked and fended it off. I'm taking evasive measures to make sure I'm not followed.

And I'm not using any Vigilante tech. It's just me and my wits.

It feels good.

I don't see anyone who would concern me on this block. A woman with a small girl on a bicycle pushes a stroller down the street. A young man in a white apron gets out of his car to go into the cafe.

I walk away from the building. I can take this residential street through the neighborhood and loop back around. It'll be obvious if anyone out of place is following.

I'm not going to be afraid. This is what I was trained for.

20

JAX

That woman is so maddening.

I race through the streets of D.C., winding my way to the townhouse complex. The tracker on Mia is on my windshield. She's only a few blocks away from home, zigzagging through the surrounding neighborhood.

I punch in the code for Sam. He's actually nearer to her than I am, closing in on the complex. I buzz him.

"Miss me already, boss?" Sam says as his image comes onscreen. When he sees my face, he adds,

"Who peed in your chili?"

"Mia was just attacked in a civilian store," I say. "Five minutes ago. She got away and is running through the streets near the complex."

"Pass me her code and I'll track her," Sam says.

"I'd rather not put her in the system."

"Roger that," he answers. "Let me go black."

"You sure?" I ask. "That will set off the network."

"They already know I'm team Jax," Sam says. He's looking away, doing something below the level of the video screen. "This network has more holes than a Mardi Gras shirt on Fat Tuesday."

He blips out for a second, then comes back. "Off the grid," he says. "Let me collect your girl."

I transmit the code. "I'm about fifteen minutes away still."

"Don't worry about it," he says. "I'll get her. You want Colette?"

"Probably," I tell him. "But she's half a day away."

"Late to the party is still a party," he says.

He drives along for a moment. "I got a visual," he says.

"She look okay?" I ask.

"Right as rain." The blur of light changes, so I know he's stopping. I hear the hum of his window coming down.

"Hey, pretty lady. Need a ride?" he says.

"Sam!"

The sound of Mia's voice calms me. I watch Sam's face as he turns, probably to watch Mia cross in front of his car. The door opens and closes.

Then her face is next to his. "Hello, Jax!" she says merrily, as if she hasn't just run from an attack.

"We're going to go find some food," Sam says. "Don't wait up."

"Like hell you are," I fire at them.

They both laugh.

"See you at the townhouse," Sam says. "Lighten up. Your girl kicks ass."

The screen blinks out.

I try to bring it down. I have the chip from Katya in my pocket. We'll go from there once I'm home.

I don't cloak the car until I'm a mile from the complex. Then I take it down to black, pulling out my off-grid device to open the gates.

Sam's olive-green jeep is parked in front of his house. He and Mia are sitting on his porch on a wide swing. Drinking iced tea, it looks like. I don't bother putting the Aston Martin in a garage, but stop in front of our house across the street.

When I get out, Sam lifts his glass. "Come and drink some N'Orleans sweet tea!" he calls out.

I close the door to the car and stride up the walk. "I like a little tea with my sugar," I say gruffly.

Mia is curled up on her corner of the swing, her feet tucked under her. "Hey, Jax."

They are just sitting here like nothing has happened. As if Mia hasn't been attacked three times in a week.

My anger threatens to boil over, but I keep it in check. "So is anyone going to tell me what happened?"

"Not while you're standing over us like a gargoyle on a church," Sam says. "I've seen winged devils that look more pleasant than you do."

"It was just some woman," Mia says. She waves her hand in the air like this is no big deal.

I perch on the edge of a cushioned wicker chair. "Was she trained? What was her attack style?"

"Civilian," Sam says. "I already asked all the pertinent questions."

"She totally freaked when I put the squeeze on her," Mia says. "Then she screamed."

"No way was that girl Vigilante trained," Sam says. "She'd have been weeded out in Phase One."

I sit back. "But the other two hits were inside jobs."

"Mia's not inside anymore," Sam says. "You took her offline. They have to get creative."

"Nobody used real people on the network jobs," Mia says. "Just tech. They don't want anybody to know what they are doing."

I open my suit jacket to dig into the breast pocket. "Your friend Katya paid me a visit." I drop the chip on the table between me and Sam. "She's been handling the data on specials in archives. Says she matched up some codes with some civilian newspaper reports. Three specials are dead in the past month. Young ones. Looks like accidents or health stuff, but it's too much, too fast."

Sam picks up the chip. "This is old school."

Mia groans. "You should see archives. It's 2010 all over again."

Sam raises his eyebrow. "You were ten years old in 2010."

Mia laughs. "I know! I used a chip just like that in school."

"I think archives needs beefing up," Sam says.

"You got something to read that?" I ask.

"Does a crawfish have a dick?" Sam says.

Both Mia and I turn to him.

"I don't know," Mia says. She wrinkles her nose. "Does it?"

Sam laughs. "Let me get my stuff from my car."

He heads down the porch steps.

I move to sit next to Mia. "Were you hurt?" I turn her head to the side. "Looks pretty red."

"It might bruise," Mia says. "I can add it to my collection."

I touch her face. "It's not swollen."

She takes my hand. "I'll survive. Got bigger lumps at the vault."

"You're really getting hammered here," I tell her.

"Part of the job description," she says. "So Katya came to see you?"

"Yes. She got worried when you disappeared. Apparently there was a flurry of deletion in the archives in the days after you left."

"Probably hiding something about the car malfunction," she says.

"That's what we're guessing." I hesitate. "Three other specials are down," I say. "One in a car accident, one in a fall, and a third of a prescription-drug overdose."

She goes still. "Civilians, then?"

"Of course," I say. "The only Vigilante special left in the network is you. There are about twenty civilian specials, including Jovana, now that she's exiled."

"This doesn't sound like Jovana's work," she says.

"I don't think so either. It's a systematic approach."

"Those poor people." Mia lays her head on my shoulder, then pops it back up. "We have to protect the others. Who are they? Where are they?"

"That's the thing," I say. "We don't track specials. That's why they are specials."

"So we can't protect them?" she asks.

"Not the way the system is now." I turn to look at Sam dragging bags and cases from his jeep. "But that chip from Katya is all the archives information she's been deleting. Looks to be all special data."

"You're going to compromise their status?" she asks.

"I think we have to."

Sam tromps up the steps with two duffels.

"Make yourself useful, boss, and grab those bags." He nudges his shoulder against his front door. When it opens, he sniffs and sighs. "Sweet Jesus, somebody's making beignets." He turns to Jax. "I love your people."

"Camryn is a great cook," I say.

"Hot damn." He dumps his bags on the floor. "Come on. Let's unload."

Mia gets up, but Sam waves her back into the swing. "You've had enough for one day. Just sit there with your tea and think happy southern thoughts."

I follow Sam down the stairs to his car. The two of us are incongruous, Sam in his jeans and sweatshirt and me in a suit. I glance back up at Mia in her casual clothes. Maybe it's time to take everything down a notch.

I loosen my tie. We'll start with this.

21

MIA

With Sam and Jax neck deep in code more boring than the stuff I sifted through in archives, I head across the street to Jax's townhouse.

I can't think of it as mine yet, or ours. Just his.

The door pops open after my scan and I flop onto the sofa. I could sleep for a million years after the stress of today. Probably not very Vigilante of me.

I'm not sure what I am now. I qualified for Vigilante status, but then Jax decommissioned me.

I'm nobody.

The wall screen blinks green in one corner. Encrypted message direct to the house.

I plan to ignore it and remain collapsed on the velvety cushions, but it nags at me. Maybe it's something Jax and Sam could be using. Or maybe it's Katya with more information.

"Wall screen, play message," I say.

The icon wings its way to the central part of the screen and opens. It's just text. From Arthur De Luca. I sit up, alert now.

The message reads:

> *Jax, bro, you're still as intense as ever. Mom and Dad are planning to come up as you asked. They'll be there in about four hours. I'm not sure about us. Sarah says the kids have some school stuff and Toby has already missed two soccer games. Apparently that's a thing.*
>
> *Maybe we can be there by the weekend. I'll let you know.*

I glance at the time stamp. Two hours ago.

Jax's parents will arrive in two hours!

My body leaps from the sofa. I look around.

Everything's spotless, of course. That gets done with the stealth of a cleaning ninja.

What do I wear?

My hand flies to my cheek. Of course, I would have a big old bruise on my face.

I've just pulled my shirt over my head when I remember that Jax may not have this message. I tap on my watch even as I race across the room, kicking off my jeans. I've gotten the bra off when Jax appears. His eyes are wide. "Now this is an excellent use of video chat."

I adjust the angle. "My eyes are up here. And your parents are going to arrive in two hours!"

He nods. "They just sent their itinerary." His eyes keep looking down, as if he expects the camera angle to go low again. "I take it you're going to shower."

I can't finish undressing without moving my arm. I slip my panties off and hurry to the bathroom. When I bring my wrist back up, Jax is coughing lightly. "That was quite the view," he says.

I look down at my naked bits. "No time for that!" I tell him. "Will you send your parents over here?"

"I think I'm about to get over there myself," he

says huskily.

I twist the water faucets. When I turn back to my wrist, I see I've given him another gawker view. "You've seen it all before," I say. "Now stall them over there until I'm ready to meet them."

His expression shows his amusement. "All right, Mia."

I hear Sam say something and the screen goes pink as Jax covers the watch with his hand. After a moment, I see Jax again. "We're getting somewhere with the data," he says. "Come over when you're ready."

I'm already in the water. "Fine, Jax," I say, soaking my hair. When I look at my wrist again, he's still there, watching.

My body warms over. Despite my panic over the imminent arrival of his family, I hesitate, watching him look at me.

"I'm jealous of that trail of water right there," he says.

I look down at the rivulet falling from my collarbone down between my breasts, and on past my belly button. My heart speeds up. "Your parents have their own house here, right?" I ask.

His eyes come back up to meet mine. His voice

is gruff. "They do."

"I'll be over soon," I say, and flick off the transmission.

As I soap my hair, I take a moment to really fall into what I'm feeling after seeing Jax's reaction to me. Hot. Excited. In love. Maybe I had been wrong to say no in Switzerland. We could be married by now. Having a normal life.

And I would have already met these parents.

I rinse out the suds. I love Jax. I know this. He's dropped everything for me, twice.

And now I am in this big mess. Maybe it's time I did things his way. He knows the Vigilantes better than I do.

Yes, I'll tell him. As soon as we figure out what all these attacks are about, I'll pull out. Spend time just with him. Like in Switzerland. Try again to grow those dang watermelons.

I shut off the spray.

My dressing room is full of Armond creations. I can look any way I want, from a state dinner to the red carpet to lounging at home. Probably I want to be close to the latter.

The button to move my clothes along the motorized rail is hidden behind a sequined gown

Armond sent when we first arrived in D.C. He assumed I might do something fancy. Not so. Mainly I'd been in training gear or mission outfits.

I push the sparkling black dress aside and move the track until I get to the jeans. I pick a serviceable pair, soft and deep blue. Then I shift the clothes again until I reach the shirts.

Keep it simple. Blue? Jax likes me in blue. Be bold? Red. Subtle? Beige.

Panic courses through me, more than when the vault blew. More than the car going berserk. Definitely more than that poorly trained martial arts girl in the bridal shop.

What if his parents don't like me? What if I'm not good enough for Jax? Too young? Too immature? Too unsophisticated? I can only imagine all the things they have seen and done. I picture a smartly dressed woman with her hair all done up, and a handsome man graying at the temples. Jax is a lot to manage already, with his impeccable taste and outrageous standards. Now I have to measure up to his parents.

I sit on the floor, staring at the clothes. Maybe I should call Armond. He could tell me what to wear.

My forehead drops to my hands. I'm tired. So

tired. I thought I really had this. Those early days with Jax, escaping security, jumping into waterfalls, blowing up land mines. I felt invincible.

But now, I just feel…incompetent. Seven tries to succeed at blowing the vault in training. Then a botched mission. Then failing to manage the car when it malfunctioned. Colette handled hers just fine.

The elation I felt after escaping the girl in the store completely evaporates. Even that wasn't handled well, I realize. She got away. Now we don't know who sent her. I should have captured her, interrogated her. I had basic training in all this. Maybe I'm not Phase Three or Four, or whatever. But she had *screamed*, for Pete's sake. I should have been able to manage her.

And I hadn't.

This misery isn't about the clothes I will wear at all. It's about how I've done nothing but fail since I tried to qualify to be a Vigilante. How Jax's parents will see that. They were Vigilantes. They know how it works. And they will realize how low Jax has stooped to choose me.

I stand up and select a soft green sweater from the shelf. It's comfortable and well made. I feel good in it. If I'm going to head over to Sam's place and face Jax's family, I might as well be dressed the way I like. They'll have to take me at face value.

22

JAX

My parents arrive precisely at the appointed hour. They have always been prompt.

I stand on Sam's porch. I haven't heard from Mia since her shower, but I tap out a quick message that they have arrived. She'll come on her schedule. I know this isn't an easy thing for her.

But they will love her. She has nothing to fear.

I should have told her that.

Mom steps out of the black Mercedes. She looks incredible, sixty-five going on forty. But she dresses like the grandmother she is. Long floral skirt.

Pinkish sweater. Flat shoes. Armond would have a fit, since she could still do a runway strut if she wanted. He would want her in something sleek and fitted. But Mom isn't into that. If you pressed her on it, she'd say she wore enough leather and bustiers in her seductress days to last four lifetimes.

I shake that image out of my head.

"Jax, baby! My little boy!" She heads up the walk with her arms out. "You have gone entirely too long without visiting!"

Sam comes up behind me and leans on one of the porch supports. "He didn't call you from prison? Jax, you're a bad son."

I want to elbow him but envelop my mother in a hug instead.

She looks up at me, hands on my cheeks. "I was terrified for you during that awful time at Ridley," she says. "Did your father tell you one of his friends got incarcerated just to watch out for you?"

I glance up at Dad, who stands on the road, looking over the complex. "No, I didn't know that. Who was it?"

"Marco something or another," she says, releasing me. "You can ask him." She tugs at my loosened tie. "You could have called."

"I didn't want you two compromised," I say. "You know how it is when you're a Vigilante on the wrong side of the network."

Dad comes up the steps. "Looks like the party is at Sam's place."

Mom releases me to press a kiss to Sam's cheek. "I smell good things coming from in there. You always have the best food."

"I aim to please," Sam says. "Jax has a killer cook, all happy to have real people to bake for."

Dad shakes my hand vigorously. "I hear your new position suits you." He glances at my loose tie. I fight the urge to straighten it again. He's perfectly groomed in slacks and a custom-tailored golf shirt. His Burberry dress shoes are polished into black mirrors.

"I tried to retire," I say. "But the network sucked me back in."

Mom turns back to me. "I hear from Arthur it was the girl."

Dad looks around. "So where is this young lady? I'll have to thank her for getting you back in the game."

I see a movement across the road and spot Mia at the top of our steps. She's in jeans and a sweater, her brown-gold hair loose around her shoulders. She looks young and lost and lovely. My heart squeezes.

"Here she comes now," I say.

Everyone's attention moves to her. She walks over with easy grace, a little tentative, absently glancing left and right as she crosses the narrow road between houses as if there might be traffic there.

"Now it's a party," Sam says.

She smiles shyly up at us as she approaches the steps. My dad is closest and takes one of her hands in both of his.

"I'm Vincent. You must be the Mia we've heard so much about," he says. He kisses her knuckles. "I hear you earned your Vigilante status a few days ago. Congratulations."

She blushes furiously. "Thank you. I see where Jax gets his exquisite taste."

Mom heads down the steps and slides her arm through the crook of Mia's elbow. "Call me Di. Let's go inside and chat. I want to hear all about your training and how everything went."

Now Mia is fairly bursting with color. I know she doesn't want to talk about that at all.

"We've got work to do," I say gruffly. "Sam and

I have been putting some data together about the specials." I open the door to Sam's townhouse. "And we're triangulating information about the woman who attacked Mia a few hours ago."

Mom stops her ascent up the stairs. "What? Somebody went after Mia?"

"Third time," Sam says. "We thought she was being targeted on her own, but now it's looking like a systematic elimination of specials in the system."

Dad rubs his hands together as if he's eager to be on a case. "Sounds intriguing."

We head through Sam's entrance. I lead the crew into the dining room to work around the large oval table. Sam has his blackout equipment set up there, creating an unmonitored space for us to work. When I close the door, the seclusion is complete, no sound or signals can escape. In addition, a stream of false information goes out to make it appear our conversations and activity can be seen and heard.

Sam is good.

"Start from the beginning," Mom says. "Why would anyone target Mia?"

I explain about her special status and some of the more private details of how the Vigilante committee literally went up in smoke over Jovana.

And that Olivia wanted the special status eliminated from the network.

"Surely Olivia Beauchamp isn't killing specials," Mom says. "She's been a loyal Vigilante for fifty years."

"It's a little too obvious for me," I say. "If you've got something to hide, you're not going to show up in my office every other day insisting I do something about it."

"Unless you're looking for a cover," Dad says. "The old girl was always shrewd."

"Here's what we've got on the one who came after Mia," Sam says. He brings a picture of the girl up on the wall monitor. Her face looms over the room.

I sense Mia draw in a breath. "How long did she watch for me?" she asks.

Sam minimizes the image and brings up video footage from the cameras on the townhouse complex walls. "Her, just today. Probably when Jax took you off grid again, they had to resort to old-school stakeouts. If we sort through the previous days, there were probably others."

"Why did they hire somebody with so little skill?" Mia asks.

Sam shrugs. "We started looking into who sent her money. She's a heavy for a local bar owner. Small stuff. Shakedowns. Bad debt." Onscreen, a starburst from the woman's picture shows the connections to other people.

Sam brings an image forward. "Now this guy, he's probably the one who paid for this gig. He's a middle man for this sort of thing."

Another starburst comes off him with his connections.

"We would have been chasing all the wild geese on this one, except one payment to this guy stood out," Sam says.

Another image comes up, a young guy in an MIT sweatshirt.

"He doesn't look very dangerous," Mom says.

"He's not," Sam says. "Clean as a whistle. But look at one of his friends."

In the starburst of this boy's connections, one of the images is bordered by red.

"He knows a Vigilante," Dad says. "So this could tie him to the person who altered the code on the inside."

"Not just any Vigilante," Sam says. He pulls up the network information for another young man.

"But a protégé of none other than Olivia Beauchamp."

The list of vital statistics scrolls up the screen.

Chet Chambers. Born 1998.

Mother: Ariel Newcomb Chambers. Born 1970. Deceased 2017. Mission P6-4529. GSW.

Father: Charles Chambers. Born 1965. Deceased 2017. Mission P6-4529. GSW.

Entered Vigilante program 2016. Area of specialty: Coding and security.

Qualifying mission passed 2016.

Phase 2 Mission passed 2016.

Phase 3 Mission passed 2016.

Phase 4 Mission passed 2017.

Phase 5 Mission failed 2017.

No further attempts.

Vigilante in good standing.

Sponsoring Vigilante: Olivia Beauchamp.

"Poor kid," Mom says. "He never went anywhere after his parents were killed on a mission."

"Maybe," I say. "He was a hotshot and rising fast. It doesn't make sense that he never tried again."

"Grief is a terrible thing," Mom says.

"For four years?" I ask. "I find it interesting that after all this time, he still hasn't tried to rise up the ranks. And if he's able to do what he did to Mia's data, he's probably at Phase Ten level, and hiding it by underachieving."

Dad taps his fingers absently on the table. "You think Beauchamp put him up to that? Kept him low level so she could use him?"

"It's a possibility," I say. "I think it's time we track him down."

"Are we headed to the silo?" Mia asks.

"He goes on shift at nine," Sam says. He pulls up the work schedule for Chet Chambers. "He's been coding the training sequences for the missions for years."

Mia sits up a little straighter. "Did he code my qualifying mission, the one with the vault?"

Sam digs around in the data, looking for Chet's work history.

Inside the listing of the training missions from two weeks ago is one without a Vigilante attached.

"That's probably Mia's," I say. "Since she's wiped from the data now."

Sam brings up the detailed information. Right there in black letters is what we're looking for. "Mission codex: Chet Chambers and Rider Filmore."

"Let's go," I say. "We can be at the silo at nine to apprehend him."

"Wait," Mom says. "How many specials have been killed?"

"Three," Sam says. "Mia would have been the fourth."

"And how recently?" Her face is drawn.

"Two weeks," Sam says. "There are still twenty, but we don't know who they are. That's why they're specials."

I know what she's thinking.

"I've already sent security for Arthur," I tell her.

Dad stands. "Who did you send?"

"Four top-notch Phase Eights," I tell him.

Mom smacks her hands down. "Not good enough for me," she says. "That's my grandbabies we're talking about." She stands up. "I'm going there myself. Call a helicopter."

I'm annoyed that she doesn't think my men are

good enough for Arthur, but I say, "I'll have my personal helicopter dispatched."

Dad kisses her on the head. "I trust you can handle Arthur, Di. I'm going to head to the silo with Jax," Dad says. "Then I'll come after you."

Mia tilts her head. "Is your brother in danger?" she asks.

Sam shifts the screen. "We can monitor his block and his work, just not his house," he says. "Right now they are at a soccer game and we can see everything as long as it's live." He turns to Jax. "Once it goes into the system, it's deleted, of course."

A video feed of kids running down the field comes up.

"There's Mike," Dad says, pointing at one of the boys in soccer gear. He glances at Mia. "My oldest grandson."

"I assure you we've got plenty of backup there," I say.

"Don't care," Mom says. She stands and jerks a phone from her bag. "I want on that helicopter inside five minutes."

"A car is on its way," I tell her.

Mia stands up, shaking her hands in

exasperation. "What are they talking about?" she asks. "Why would anyone go after Arthur?"

I motion to Sam to pack up, then I turn to her.

"My brother is a special too."

23

MIA

We divvy up our team. Sam goes on the helicopter with Jax's mother to get to Arthur. Vincent, Jax, and I head to the D.C. silo.

During the drive, Vincent uses an off-grid Identipad to load up the specs to the silo and the coding room. Jax pores over data coming up onscreen while I sit in the back and wonder if I'll be useful at all.

"He should be in a room full of non-combat Vigilantes," Jax says. "Apprehending him should be easy, but I don't want to tip him off ahead of time.

I've come across people like him. If he's gotten this far, he'll have a snake code in the system, ready to uncoil if he needs it."

"Isn't anybody checking his work?" I ask.

"Theoretically, yes," Vincent says. "There are two blind coders submitting the same code on every mission. But then again, we're sitting here with tech that defeats the Vigilantes' security." Vincent holds up the Identipad. "If you're working with the best of the best, they can outsmart the other best."

"How can anybody trust anybody?" I ask. I'm not sure the network is the organization I thought it was.

"We're in upheaval, no doubt about it," Jax says. The twinkling lights of D.C. whiz behind his head as the car auto-drives to the silo. "Been that way since Sutherland recruited Jovana, and now we're dealing with fallout."

"But killing innocent people," I say. "That's not what we've ever stood for. At least that's how I was trained."

"You're right," Vincent says. "But anytime you concentrate too much power in one spot, the whole system is at risk. We went through a similar upheaval in 1981. I was just a Phase Six designing qualifying missions, and we couldn't get anything done for all the people pushing their own agendas."

"Stupid amount of American politicians got caught up in that," Jax says. "Blood spilling on national television and Vigilantes caught on camera."

"We learned from it," Vincent says. "And we'll learn from this."

"So the plan is just to surprise him?" I ask.

"Can't count on it. The whole silo might light up just from me entering the facility off schedule," Jax says.

"My presence will help," Vincent says. "Family visits don't seem too threatening."

"Little do they know," Jax says and laughs.

"We've never done a job together," Vincent says.

"Certainly not against our own network," Jax adds.

"It'll be fun," Vincent says.

I sit in the backseat, just listening and learning. Jax is actually *laughing*. They don't seem too worried about picking up a coding specialist inside a high-security silo. Like this will be a walk in the park.

But I know that an untrained girl in stolen shoes managed to get out of one. Of course, I did have my special status, so I could move around. But this guy writes the code that runs things. There is no telling what he has access to.

"Will the silo go on lockdown?" I ask.

"The minute we pass inside," Jax says. "But I'm not going to rely on that."

"Can he escape?" I ask. "If he runs?"

"Not easily," Jax says. "My security should override anything he does, but he might be really good."

"All right," Vincent cuts in. "Looks like the best way to do this is to go in like normal, take me around, and let everyone see you're just showing me your new digs. It will be like a tour."

He points to part of the map. "Only when we're here, level three, do you bring in any outside security and tip our hand. I'd say six of your best evasive-combat guards. And when we're here"—he stabs the screen—"inside the coding room, we act. I'd go straightforward, dart gun."

Jax taps on his monitor, pulling up the images of Vigilantes on duty and dragging them to varying spots on the silo map. "Good so far," Jax says.

Vincent glances back at me. "Mission design. I love this stuff."

I nod. It is fascinating, watching him actually put things in place. Ever since I've been with Jax, we seem to always run in without a plan and react by our wits.

"He'll know we're on to him as soon as we're in the room," Vincent says. "You have weapons here? If we take any on site, he might have code alerting him. He's probably been watching all sorts of activity since he began this assault."

"I've got six darts in the back. Two guns." Jax glances back at me. "What's Mia's role?"

"Arm yourself and her," Vincent says. "I'm just the retired folk. Don't need the scans picking up an old man with an unauthorized dart."

The car pulls up to the silo.

Jax turns around. "Open interior trunk access," he tells the car. Then to me, "Might want to scoot over."

I shift to the side as a panel drops down in the middle of the backseat.

"You should be able to access the darts," Jax says.

I reach through the panel and pull the box onto

the seat. "Which ones should we load?" I ask.

"Neuro," Vincent says. "The gut ones don't incapacitate quickly enough. And leave the antidotes. There are plenty of those inside. We should go light."

I'm glad for my training as I load the two guns with blue darts. At least I'm competent at this. I pass one up to Jax. This is the first time I've felt like a real Vigilante.

"I'm still a special, right?" I ask. "It might make sense for me to carry both in since I'm not tracked."

"Smart girl," Vincent says.

"I'm head of syndicate," Jax says. "I am also a silent track."

"Of course," I say.

"Ready for this?" Vincent asks me.

I nod. I tuck the dart gun into the band of my jeans near my front hip. I wish for a Vigilante uniform and its pockets and holsters, but this look is right for a casual tour. At least I'm not wearing breakneck heels and a miniskirt.

We exit the car and wait for it to take off for vehicle storage. Then we approach the main entrance.

The scan here is invisible, but the doors part for

us. Two guards nod at Jax and separate to let us by.

We pass through the glass hall. Jax's HEAD OF SYNDICATE notation fills his wall. No other information is displayed.

Along Vincent's path is his image and vitals. His last known location is a wine shop near the townhouse. Jax's home location is skipped. The blackout there is serious. "Picked up a little libation for dinner," Vincent says to the woman overseeing the data. "Didn't figure on a silo stop."

His outline walks along the wall beside him with two pulsing colors glowing near his waist.

"Vigilante-issue blade and dart guard," the woman says to one of the guards.

"It's just my father," Jax says. "He's come to look at where I work."

"Bring your dad to work day," Vincent says with a chortle.

The woman and the guard review Vincent's record of service and background. Finally, they wave him through.

My wall is just like the silo entrances were before I went into training. My name, MIA MORROW, and nothing else. Not even a picture. Like Jax, I don't have a scanned outline showing my weapons and tech.

I walk to join Jax and Vincent.

"Haven't been in this silo in a decade," Vincent says. "Looks good." We head down the curving stairs into the hub. "How many levels? Ten?" he asks, as if he hasn't just been studying the map in the car for twenty minutes.

"More or less," Jax says. He waves to the night-duty information techs manning the glass screens. "We have a light crew in the evenings."

"Looks like a helluva lot of people to me," Vincent says. "The Miami syndicate didn't have anywhere near this level of personnel."

"It's a busy place," Jax says.

They keep talking this way as we head to the stairwell that will take us down into the silo's guts.

"Still hate elevators, I see," Vincent says. He turns to me. "Ever since that gas incident in '06."

I want to hear more about this, but the stairwell door pops open with Jax's scan.

Once we're inside, the chatter stops. I wonder if I should pass the dart gun to Vincent, but I don't say anything.

Jax checks his watch. "Everyone's ready to move in," he says.

"Let's head to three," Vincent says.

But when we get to that level, the door is shut tight. "Manual scan," Jax says to the box.

But it's off.

"Snakes in the code," Vincent says. "Just like you called it."

We go down another level in case Chet has only blocked his own. This one is also shut tight.

Jax taps his watch and flicks to scroll through updates. "The silo is in lockdown," he says. "He can't get out. I'll send the external security to the exit doors."

His watch buzzes back.

"Getting through?" Vincent asks. His voice is tight.

"So far," Jax says. "He can't have the snakes everywhere. Too much rogue code would get intercepted."

"He'll try to contain us and make an escape," Vincent says. "So he will have prioritized the scans, the doors, and any areas he had access to."

"How did he know we were here?" I ask.

"No telling," Vincent says. "Could be Jax coming in late. Could be you. Could be he heard from the girl who attacked you."

"Doesn't matter now," Jax says.

We go down one more level.

Still locked.

"Are we trapped in here?" I ask. The stairwell is wide and well lit, but it's still uncomfortable to think that we're stuck.

"I can have a door blown from the other side," Jax says. "We just have to choose a level."

"We don't know where he is," Vincent says.

We continue down. At level ten, a light glows not from the silo side, but from a door down a short concrete hall.

I know this one well. "It's the training facility," I say. I practically lived on level ten while I was preparing for the vault mission.

"Makes sense," Vincent says. "This is where he controls all the code."

"I don't like it," Jax says. "He's got a full complement of weapons and tech in that stronghold."

"Plus the loading-deck riser goes straight topside," Vincent says. "You think he can get out that way?"

"It's quite possible he coded that one to let him out even during lockdown." He taps his watch. "Full armor to training loading-deck exit."

"Won't be fast enough. He might already be out," Vincent says.

The green light beckons. Jax approaches, but when it scans him, a blast of red lines crisscross the pod.

"Nice," Vincent says. "Do all the pods have lasers?"

"All the ones leading to silo exits do," Jax says.

Vincent approaches. The red beams remain.

Jax steps away, speaking low into his watch.

I approach the door to examine the beams. I turn the hem of my sweater under and pull out a loose thread. I toss it into the lasers.

A tiny wisp of smoke lifts from where the string hits the beam.

I take a step closer. The scan crosses me and the beams wink out.

"Hey," I say. I step into the pod.

"Mia!" Jax says, but the door has already opened for me. I turn around as it closes and the red beams return to keep Jax and Vincent out.

But I'm in.

The training dock is semi-lit, closed up for the night. There's a bank vault set up, just like when I trained. This one is different, though, shorter and more squat. The hall dimensions are different too. I walk up to the metal wall and run a finger along the cool surface.

A light clicks on above me. It's the observation room where AnneMarie watched me fail. But it isn't AnneMarie up there.

It's the man from the image Sam showed us.

Chet.

He leans into the mike. "I see we have a special in the house."

I glance back at the entrance pod. No doubt Vincent and Jax are completely freaking out on the other side.

"I did my mission training here," I say. "Was feeling nostalgic."

"How did the blast go?" he asks.

"Kept blowing it," I say with a laugh. "And myself." I point to my ear. "Might have permanent damage."

"Not an easy thing to master," he says.

He's so calm, I almost wonder if he knows we're on to him.

"What are you doing down here?" I ask. "Do you code missions?" I point to the vault. "Looks like somebody is finishing the job I messed up."

"Yeah, that counterfeiting operation moved on. Another operative will take it down." He isn't looking at me, but working frantically on a monitor I can't quite see.

For a moment, I wonder if we have it wrong. If the problems with the stairwell were unrelated. Chet really does look like he's just doing his work.

I keep walking. I know there is a hallway off one end, where the trainers meet. Farther down is the big storage with everything from vault doors to fire escapes to armored cars, all ready to be brought into training as needed. A smaller storage room has an armory of explosives, guns, and tech for practice.

"Where you headed, special?" Chet asks.

"Just looking at all the places that were home to me for a while," I say casually.

"I can't let you go any farther," he says.

My heart speeds up a notch, but I breathe evenly. "Am I disturbing your work?"

"This silo's on lockdown, and you're my key to getting out of here."

So he knows.

He hasn't moved from his position in the observation room. I'm not sure what he can do from there. I shrug and head toward the hall anyway.

I'm only one step in when red lasers cross my path. I jump back.

"I told you," Chet says. "You're not leaving here."

My watch buzzes. It's a message from Jax on our secure channel.

Chet is bargaining your life for his freedom. Are you all right?

I tap the watch once for yes. I turn back to the main room.

"How is the latest training going?" I ask. "Are they getting this vault blown?"

Chet laughs. "It's easy work if someone isn't screwing with the data."

My face flames hot. I look up at him. "Were you the reason I couldn't blow the vault in all those tries?"

"I may have underpowered your blast a few times so that you'd overcompensate," he says. "You're tougher than you look. That blast on the mission should have taken you out, especially without the planter to shield you. It never existed."

I breathe carefully to maintain my calm. "Well, it's for the best," I say. "I'm just going to get married and have babies anyway."

This gets him. "You're giving up being a Vigilante?"

I shrug. "Wasn't for me."

I wander around the vault again, looking for anything I can use against him. I have a dart gun, but he's behind a blast-proof window. Maybe I can get in the observation room somehow. The side door will certainly be locked. But if he wants to use me as bait, he'll need to be closer.

Staying calm is priority one. I examine the vault. This one is pristine, no burn marks pointing to attempted blows. I know for a fact that the first pass on the explosion is always low so you can get your timing down.

So there should be a mark if it's been used at all. If not, then the green vial should still be —

Yes. Stuck to the inner frame. I spot it but walk on by. Chet may code these missions but he isn't there when they are tested. He doesn't know where the tools are placed as an operative is taken through the steps. He also may not realize that while his window is technically blast proof, an extra barrier slides into place over it during an actual explosion. I've seen it open and close a dozen times during my own training.

I pass the cylinder again, making sure it's not just a dummy. The liquid inside shines. It's real, all right.

I don't have any electronics to blow it with precision. But an explosion is an explosion. All that has to happen is that the chemicals mix. The fancy plug-ins are just to control the timing and intensity.

Chet continues to work the monitor up in the room. I wonder if he's talking to Jax. If they are moving out security to let him go. I wouldn't think so. Jax would have enough faith in me, I think, to let me try to apprehend him.

But then, I just ran after the attack at the bridal shop. And I didn't exactly show exemplary skill on either of my missions.

Chet stands. "Your boyfriend is being reasonable. You and I are about to take a little trip to the outside."

Jax? Reasonable. I doubted it. Anything he said or did with Chet would have an angle.

But I wasn't in on that and didn't have time to ask.

Choice time. Blow the observation window, or try? Or wait until he gets close to me and dart him? I watch him pick up a bag inside the observation room. He takes out a dart gun of his own.

So it might be like the Wild West. Who is the quicker draw? Would he get me or I get him? Or would we get each other and both die in seven minutes?

I look at the green vial. The explosive might not blow the window straight on, but there is a small opening near the upper corner where the speaker transmits the sound into the chamber. It's the weak point in the wall, normally covered by the sliding shield during testing.

Chet glances at his monitor one more time and I know it's time to act.

24

JAX

It's all I can do to keep from exploding.

Ten minutes have passed since Mia entered the test facility. That little bastard Chet has been sending messages to us constantly, trying to exchange his freedom for Mia's life. I know my channel to Mia is clean, but I don't risk using it too often in case he notices. Mia's only message was a terse affirmative. I'm trusting she responded truthfully, and wasn't just trying to reassure me.

My Blackphone buzzes. Chet has sent a voice recording.

"Okay, De Luca, this is how it goes. Morrow and I will be exiting soon. I am armed. Type-A neurotoxin. Quick and painless, and you won't have time to figure out which one before it kicks in. If I catch a whiff of Vigilantes, she dies. Signal your understanding within thirty seconds."

I run through another round of calming mental exercises to keep my focus. I catch myself tugging at my cuffs again. If my father notices the habit, he does not say anything. Instead he stares at the Identipad, his brow furrowed as his fingers dance over its surface. "Got twenty seconds to update before I respond," I say.

"We can only put one team near the loading bay without him spotting them," Dad says. "It's not optimal, but a second can work as backup from an observation point on this building here. Any other location is too visible."

"Intentional," I say. "Can't allow anyone easy access to an ambush."

"Just stating a fact."

He sounds tense. Belatedly I realize he was just thinking out loud. I leave him to his work. He's in his element now, and anything I say will only distract him.

I call up the silo head of security on my Blackphone. "What's the status on gaining access to the training facility?"

"I think we may almost have an override in place," he says, his voice firm but controlled. "But it's tricky. There's another worm attached to the snake code, and we don't know what it does." He pauses. "I'd say another five minutes."

"We don't have five minutes," I say, holding my voice neutral.

"We could kill the code now and risk the worm."

He leaves the implied threat unsaid. The worm could do anything. Blow a set of explosives. Flood a room with gas. Chet's reach into the silo is limited, but he doesn't need it if Mia is in the line of fire.

Damn it.

"Do what you can without triggering the worm," I say. Then I send a terse message to Chet.

Understood.

It takes all my self-control not to throw my Blackphone at the wall.

"Jax," my father says. "It's not your fault. He's not free yet. And there's still Mia."

"I do not need the reminder," I say, but he is

right. This reaction is driven by not just my anger at Chet but my fear for Mia's safety.

But Mia is no ordinary woman. She has more raw talent than I've seen in a decade. She thinks on her feet. She defeated land mines with hay bales.

She took out Sutherland, in the most secure facility in North America.

A sense of calm spreads over me. After another moment, I almost feel sorry for Chet. He isn't going to know what hit him.

A vibration rolls through the floor, followed almost immediately by the dull thump of an explosive charge. Dad and I look at each other. My Blackphone chimes, and my watch buzzes.

"Explosion within the training facility!" reads the message.

I send a message to Mia on our secure channel, but get no response. Anger surges.

"Jax!" Dad's voice cuts through my mental haze. "The scanner. It's dark. It should be in emergency override!"

I look toward the entrance pod. Both the beams and the green scanning light are off. I rush to it, but the door does nothing. No scan, no movement. I rip open a panel on the side and pass my watch over it.

A low tone sounds. It's in override.

A secondary panel opens with a good old-fashioned keypad. I type in the numbers only I know and the pod doors slide open. The training room beyond is cast in murky half light. Smoke drifts in lazy wisps near the ceiling. I can smell the acrid tinge of the training explosives hanging in the air.

My father is right behind me as I dash inside. "Mia!" I call out. "Where are you?"

We turn and find ourselves in one of the rooms mocked up like the counterfeiter's base of operations. The big steel vault door is unblemished, but the blast-proof observation glass high on the wall hangs partly out of its reinforced frame, a large hole adjacent to it. The room beyond is dark, save for the red glow of emergency lighting outlining a single figure.

"Mia?"

The figure inside moves. A second later Mia's face appears in the hole. "Jax! Get in here! I've opened the side door."

Relief floods through me as Dad and I run around. The observation room is a scene of chaos and destruction. Judging by the condition of the glass and the location of the hole, Mia must have found a weak spot and dumped one hell of a load on it. The wall, designed to reflect shock waves rather than absorb them, crumpled like balsa wood.

That's my girl.

Mia crouches by a figure on the floor. Her dart gun lies at her feet nearby. I drop down next to her and look at Chet. His eyes are open but glassed over. Thin rivulets of blood trickle from his nostrils and ears. Dust hangs in the air and debris lies everywhere.

A large, twisted shard of metal wall stud protrudes from his chest. He's propped halfway on his side due to the size of it. His shirt is soaked in a growing crimson stain.

My Blackphone vibrates again but I ignore it. "Trauma team to the training facility," I say into my watch.

I reach out and lay a hand under his jaw. Chet's pulse is weak and flutters like a helpless moth under my finger.

"Operative Chambers," I call out, and wave a hand in front of his face. "Chet. Can you understand me? Do you see me?"

Chet's eyes shift to the side, but I'm not sure they focus on anything. He mouths something, but no sound comes out.

"We're getting medical in," I tell him. I look back up at Mia. "Are you hurt?"

"I was shielded by the vault," she says.

I spot blood on her wrist. "What's that?" I ask, pointing.

"Just from jumping up the wall and climbing in," she says. "It's nothing."

I look back down at Chet. His lungs suck in a breath, but the gurgling sound points to a punctured lung.

Dad kneels down. "Did you act alone, Chet?"

Footsteps sound below. I stand up. Four combat guards rush into the training facility below, followed by two medics with a stretcher.

"Up here," I shout.

Two of the guards burst into the observation room, guns at the ready.

"Stand down," I say. "He's seriously injured."

They move aside for the medics.

Mia gets out of the way. I reach for her and pull her close. "Good call," I whisper in her ear.

"I didn't mean to hurt him," she says.

"He tried to kill you three times," I remind her. "He had no intention of letting you go at any point."

"I know," she says.

The medics call in for assistance to try to cut down the metal protruding from Chet. They do their best to work around it, checking his vitals and placing a mask over his nose and mouth.

A wail draws our attention to the door. Olivia Beauchamp stands there, her panicked eyes on the scene.

"What have you done to my boy?"

Dad and I exchange glances. How could she have known he was here?

She pushes past the guards and lowers herself painfully to her knees beside him. Her gray knit pants soak with blood. She takes his hand. "What happened?"

"He was trying to use Mia as a hostage to escape," I tell her.

"Why would sweet Chet need to escape? I was just coming to visit him on shift." She blinks her tears so that they fall on Chet's shirt. The medics try to shift him to see if there is a way to move him to the stretcher.

"We tied him back to a payment for a civilian hit on Mia," I tell her, mainly to judge her reaction. "We have reason to believe he was after specials."

"Oh no, oh no, oh no," she moans. "He was so devoted to me. He knew I was opposed to specials." She looks up at me with wounded eyes. "He thought he was doing it for me."

A machine beeps a warning.

"He's coding," one of the medics says. He unloads a box from the end of the stretcher. "I need everyone to stand clear." He pulls Olivia's hand from Chet's. "I'm sorry, ma'am. I need to help him."

She lets go. I pull Mia aside. Dad stands close to the door by the guards.

The Vigilantes have the very best medical technology, but there is only so much that can be done when you have metal through your lungs. Mia turns in to me as they work, but each shock to his chest makes more blood pour from his body.

Another medic arrives with a laser saw to cut through the metal stud, but the two on the floor wave him away. "He's not going to survive this," one says.

Olivia wails. I would like to believe her grief and her story, but it's too convenient that she's here. I assume she wanted to ensure he didn't confess that she was involved.

Still, she obviously did feel something for the boy. As the medics take their instruments away, she kneels again, almost falling. She takes his hand and presses it to her heart.

I decide to leave her alone with her grief. I take Mia by the elbow, and we leave the observation room. A battalion of guards and medics and personnel are assembled now.

"The situation is contained," I tell them. "Thank you for your work here today."

I pull Mia on through the crowd.

"You think this ends it?" she asks.

Dad strides behind us. "Nobody came to his aid. He had no other inside help. It all points to his own doing."

"Maybe he really did do it on his own," Mia says.

We pass through the entrance pod. "If Olivia is going to pin it on him, then that's the way it will go," I say. "But she'll be investigated, and I'll insist on her stepping down from the committee. Once she's deactivated, she won't have any power over anyone here."

"She'll still hate specials," Mia says.

"She can hate them on civilian time," I tell her.

We head into the stairwell.

Dad sighs. "What goes down, must walk up."

"Take the elevator," I tell him.

He holds up his hands. "I'm not dead yet."

We head up a couple flights. I think about Arthur, and whether I feel positive he's safe now.

I pause to ask Dad, "What would you do?"

He doesn't hesitate. "Compromise the specials. Protect them for a while. Keep those cards close to your chest. See what comes of it."

I turn back to the stairs. "All right."

Mia keeps up with me as we climb back to the surface. "Chet told me he deliberately sabotaged my training blasts," she says. "And the mission."

"You going back into the network, then?" My thoughts flicker briefly on the deep storage. Her ring.

"Of course!" she says. "I'm a serious badass!"

Dad chortles at this. "You've got your hands full, son," he says.

I take Mia's hand and weave our fingers together. We ascend the stairs side by side. "I really do."

Epilogue

MIA

After suffering through three days of Vigilante meetings, Jax and I finally break free to go visit Arthur and Jax's parents. Changes have definitely come. The committee is revamped. Olivia Beauchamp is forced to retire and stripped of her access to Vigilante data, the best we can do as high ranking as she is. Chet Chambers is laid to rest alongside his parents.

Jax takes his father's advice and releases the identity of the specials to a new class of Vigilantes. Katya is moved to the starter division as head of their information protection. I'm there to exchange her mint-green archives uniform for a sleek slate-blue version. She promises to forward anything useful about my history to me.

Then, we're away. I convince Jax to pack nothing but jeans and sweatshirts. I hold up a filmy sapphire negligee as bait. A sixty-five-foot coil of bondage rope dyed to match seals the deal.

The day is bright and cold as we drive up. The tree leaves along the route to the suburbs of Boston are brilliantly red and gold. I've never seen anything like it in the South.

As soon as Jax's car pulls up to a nondescript two-story house, a pair of young boys burst out the door and run down the sidewalk.

Jax rolls down the window, all smiles.

"Uncle Jax! Uncle Jax!" The boys climb through the window onto his lap. One sits there, pretending to drive the car. I guess he's about four. The other, a little older, crawls into the backseat and cries out, "I'm the bad guy! Take me to jail!"

This makes me wonder what they've told the boys about Jax's occupation. Or their grandparents', for that matter.

If Jax is still tense over the events of the past

week, he doesn't look it now, showing the little boy where to put his hands on the wheel. He's relaxed. Attentive.

"Are you special ops too?" the boy in the back asks me. "Are you going to put me in handcuffs?"

I turn to the boy. I see a little of Vincent in him, and a hint of Jax. But his hair is lighter and his cheeks more round.

"I just might!" I tell him. I press a button on the monitor in front of us. A belt snakes across the seat and locks him down.

"Ho, ho!" Jax says. "The bad guy is caught!" He turns the younger boy around to look. "Mia got him good!"

"This is wicked!" the boy says, plucking at the belt. "It did it by itself!"

Jax opens his door and steps out with the younger boy on his arm. "You going to let him go or take him to the slammer?" he asks me.

"I don't know." I look the boy in the eye. "He seems pretty villainous to me."

"How about time off for good behavior?" the boy asks. "And I can share my dessert!"

"Sold!" I say, and press the button to retract the belt. "So what is your name, criminal mastermind?"

"I'm Toby," he says. "Are you going to marry my uncle Jax?"

My mouth drops open. I look over at Jax, but he holds up his free hand in innocence. "I didn't put him up to it, I swear!" he says.

Toby crawls to the front and goes out Jax's door. I get out myself. The street is so normal. Bicycles on lawns. Hedges and fall flowers and signs for lost pets.

Vincent and Di come out on the porch. Next to them is another couple. The man must be Arthur, Jax's brother. I can sort of see it. They have a similar build, although he takes more after his mother, with his lighter hair and less chiseled features.

Toby runs ahead. "Mom! Dad! Uncle Jax is here!"

"I see that," Arthur says. "Did you get arrested?"

"There was this wicked seat belt in the back! It worked by itself!"

I follow Jax up the walk, feeling shy all over again. This is more family than I've ever seen in one spot, having only my two parents until I was eight, and then only Aunt Bea.

"Come in, Mia," Arthur says. "I've been dying

to meet you."

We enter a big front room filled with well-worn furniture and strewn with toys. The younger woman approaches. "I promise I picked up an hour ago. I'm Sarah, Arthur's wife. So nice to meet you. We were wondering if Jax was ever going to bring a girl home."

Jax's expression goes dark, and I want to laugh at his annoyance.

"He's not an easy catch, that's for sure," I say.

"I need a snack!" Toby says, dashing down the hall.

"Excuse me," Sarah says. She takes the younger boy from Jax and follows Toby. "No sugar!" she calls out. "Granola bar or cheese stick."

Arthur holds out his hands. "Family life. Nothing like your jet-set days of danger and intrigue."

We all head into a sunny kitchen.

"Show Mia the roses," Jax's dad tells Arthur.

I glance over at Jax. He gives me an encouraging half smile. "Go on," he says.

I follow Arthur out the back door in confusion. I've only been there two minutes, and they're sending me outside.

"Don't look so worried," Arthur says. "Jax has a lot more bite than I do."

I follow him along a set of round tiles that lead to the rosebushes in the back corner. "I can see the family resemblance," I say.

"I can see yours too."

I halt. "What are you talking about?"

"I met your parents once, off the coast of Miami." He pauses in front of the flowers.

"When?" I ask. My heart hammers.

"Around 2008. A little project involving dolphins. Dad got me on board after I finished my bioengineering degree."

"That's the year they died," I say.

He nods. "I was there. A lot of good people went down that day."

"Did you … see them?"

"No. I wasn't actually on the offshore rig that was doubling as the base of operations. I was a mile out when it exploded." He plucks a fading flower from a bush. "But Jax says the special archives are opening. They might leak information out now." He glances up at me. "I just wanted you to know I'm here if you want to compare facts."

"Is this why you're a special?" I ask.

"Nobody ever knows exactly why they are specials," he says. "I just know that even if you turn the Vigilantes down, sometimes they come to you."

He heads back to the house. "I'm glad you're here," he says. "I think you'll be really good for Jax."

My mind buzzes as we head back into the kitchen. The information about my parents' death is in the archives. I want to call Katya. Maybe if I give her enough information, she can help me find it. After all, she's in charge of special data now. That means *my* data.

Except, I'm still decommissioned. I'm not a Vigilante proper with clearance to look at their data.

I look up at Jax. He comes forward to take my hand.

"You're outnumbered," Vincent says to Arthur. "Not too late to join the network."

"Actually," Arthur retorts, "Mia only evened the score." He gestures to his wife and two boys. "Four to four."

"Technically I'm not even—" I start to say, but Jax interrupts me.

"Mia is going to be a great asset to the network," he says. "She'll receive a new assignment shortly."

"Is she going to be at your silo?" Di sounds alarmed that maybe I'm going to disappear.

He pulls me close. "Doesn't matter. I'm going wherever she goes."

"And give up your head of syndicate title?" Vincent asks.

"If need be," Jax says.

My belly warms over. He's been willing to go anywhere I wanted, do anything that helped me. I feel very bold as I ask him, "Did you still have a question for me? I don't think I've given you an answer."

For once, Jax can't control his expression. His eyebrows lift. "The necessary equipment is locked in the silo."

The way he says it, like the engagement ring is a dart gun or an Identipad, makes me laugh out loud. I wrap my arms around him, really appreciating the feel of his strong body in the casual clothes. No suit. No layers. He's perfect.

"Should we fetch it?" I ask.

"You sure?" He doesn't seem to believe me.

"If you're talking about what I think you're talking about, we should be celebrating!" Vincent asks.

"Yes, Jax, if that is your Vigilante code talk, you suck at it," Arthur adds. "Come on, I think we have some champagne buried in the fridge."

"Maybe behind the applesauce," Sarah says.

Arthur moves deeper into the kitchen. Jax and I sit close together on a pair of chairs at the breakfast table.

"Did you request any particular kind of assignment?" Jax's mother asks.

I shrug. "I didn't even know I was getting one."

"It's already in your message queue," Jax says. "I approved it this morning."

My heart hammers as I glance at my watch. It would be rude to look at that right now, while Arthur is searching for six matching flutes and we're about to toast an engagement, ring or no ring.

Vincent hands me a glass. "To Mia and Jax!" he says.

Jax touches his flute to mine. "To Mia," he says.

The others clink glasses with happy chatter. Even the boys bang their juice boxes together.

But my head's not quite in it. My assignment. What will it be? And where?

Jax notices my expression. "Go ahead," he says. "Take a look."

I don't need any more encouragement. I tap my watch to load the messages in my secure account. I see the one that reads "Phase Two assignment," but before I can open it, I spot another just beside it. It says, "Miami rig explosion: Declassified."

It's from Katya.

Miami.

My parents.

I choose it instead.

Dolphin Bay Incident. 2008. Seventy-six dead. Forty-two Vigilantes.

Perpetrators: Identities unknown.

My eyes can't stop staring at the last line.

Perpetrators: Identities unknown.

Despite the power of this network, the reach it has, the information, the technology, they don't know who set off the explosion that killed my parents.

But they don't feel what I feel. A searing heat in my chest makes me want to tear through the archives, leave no stone unturned, take down anyone who was involved. It's not a job to me. Not an assignment.

It's personal.

I sip my champagne and glance up at Jax. He's smiling at me, assuming I'm reading about my first official Vigilante assignment.

But I know where I'm going instead.

Miami.

*The Vigilantes Series will continue
as Mia does more missions!*

Join the mail list to make sure
you don't miss a release!

www.anniewinters.com

If you love Annie's writing style, check out her books under her pen names:

USA Today bestselling **JJ Knight** for suspense serials grounded in the real world (no spies!)

USA Today bestselling **Deanna Roy** for standalone emotional romances without cliffhangers.

www.ingramcontent.com/pod-product-compliance
Lightning Source LLC
Chambersburg PA
CBHW020318200626
46814CB00006BA/2297